"I find you overbearing ...and phony!"

Sara didn't mince words when she spoke to Benedict. He wasn't pleased, yet he said calmly, "Overbearing I may be, but I'm not phony, and I want us to be friends."

"Why?"

"Why does any man want to be friends with a beautiful woman?"

"Generally to get her into bed!" said Sara so bluntly that he laughed.

"I'm not saying it hasn't crossed my mind, but it isn't my prime motive. I'm curious to see how long you'll intrigue me," Benedict replied.

Appalled at his conceit, Sara said, "I'll intrigue you as long as I continue to resist you."

"I'm noted for my staying power, Sara...."

ROBERTA LEIGH wrote her first book at the age of nineteen and since then has written more than seventy romance novels, as well as many books and film series for children. She has also been an editor of a woman's magazine and produced a teen magazine, but writing romance fiction remains one of her greatest joys. She lives in Hampstead, London, and has one son.

Books by Roberta Leigh

HARLEQUIN PRESENTS

461—CONFIRMED BACHELOR
819—NO TIME FOR MARRIAGE
954—MAID TO MEASURE
1026—A RACY AFFAIR
1043—TOO BAD TO BE TRUE
1066—AN IMPOSSIBLE MAN TO LOVE

HARLEQUIN ROMANCE

1424—THE VENGEFUL HEART
1695—MY HEART'S A DANCER
1715—IN NAME ONLY
1783—CINDERELLA IN MINK
1800—SHADE OF THE PALMS
1893—IF DREAMS CAME TRUE

Don't miss any of our special offers. Write to us at the following address for information on our newest releases.

Harlequin Reader Service
901 Fuhrmann Blvd., P.O. Box 1397, Buffalo, NY 14240
Canadian address: P.O. Box 603,
Fort Erie, Ont. L2A 5X3

ROBERTA LEIGH

no man's mistress

Harlequin Books

TORONTO • NEW YORK • LONDON
AMSTERDAM • PARIS • SYDNEY • HAMBURG
STOCKHOLM • ATHENS • TOKYO • MILAN

Harlequin Presents first edition July 1988
ISBN 0-373-11092-8

Original hardcover edition published in 1987
by Mills & Boon Limited

CHAPTER ONE

As Sara James wiped the stage make-up from her face and ran a comb through her thick amber-coloured hair, she knew that if she had any sense she'd start looking for another job. Damn it, she'd earn more scrubbing the boards than singing on them! Her mother was right: trying to make it as an opera singer was a hopeless dream.

Yet she wasn't ready to wake up from it, she admitted ruefully as she went down to the stage door, where a tall, fair-haired man in his late twenties was waiting for her.

'Which three-star take-away shall it be tonight?' he asked in a surprisingly deep voice. 'Chinese, Chinese or Chinese?'

'Chinese, I think!' she said solemnly, linking her arm through his as they went out into the cold northern night.

'At least there's one good thing about playing in a one-horse town,' he remarked jauntily. 'It saves you making decisions!'

'What puts you in such a good mood?' she asked.

He did not answer until he was sitting opposite her in the humid atmosphere of the late-night café, when he confessed he was returning to London to audition for another job.

Sara did not hide her dismay. She and Colin had worked together, on and off, since their student days, and he was her closest friend.

'It means a change of career,' he went on, 'but staying with this company is a dead end.'

'You're not giving up singing!'

'Don't be daft! All I'm doing is changing my tune.'

'What does that mean?' Her large grey-green eyes, fringed with such long dark lashes they looked false, narrowed with speculation.

'I've got the chance of a part in the new Benedict Peters show.'

'But that's a musical!' she exclaimed.

'Which means I'll get paid a decent wage for a change! Don't be a snob, Sara. The man's a first-rate composer.'

'Which is why he should be ashamed of himself wasting his talent writing such lightweight stuff.'

'Not every composer sees himself as Wagner! That's as short-sighted as saying every painter should paint like Rembrandt! Variety's the spice of life, old girl.'

'OK, you've made your point,' Sara conceded.

'Then prove it by letting me fix up an audition for *you*.'

'No, thanks. I'd never want to sing in anything that man wrote.'

'Why not?' Colin regarded her suspiciously. 'You make it sound very personal.'

'It is.' She was sorry the instant she had spoken, but it was too late to retract what she had said. 'He's not my type,' she added lamely.

'From which I gather you know him?'

'Of course not. But . . .'

'But what? Come on, out with it. I've heard he's quite a Lothario.'

'Which is why I can't stand him. No, not because of anything he did to me, but——' She stopped again. 'Look, let's change the subject.'

'I'm not letting you off the hook as easily as that! You started the story, so the least you can do is finish it.'

'It isn't my story to tell.'

'Have a heart, Sara!'

Realising that by remaining silent she would arouse his curiosity the more, she gave in. 'This is between you and me, Colin. I don't want it going any further.'

'I give you my word.'

She hesitated, then said: 'Remember my friend Barbie

Lomax—the girl who broke her hip in a car crash a few months ago?'

'Sure I do. Wasn't her fiancé driving at the time?'

'Yes, he was. But he's not her fiancé any longer. The swine ditched her a week after she was taken to hospital.'

'Nice guy! But where does Peters——'

'He's the one!'

'You're kidding! What a match! How come you never mentioned it before?'

'I never knew before,' Sara said swiftly. 'Barbie's in the middle of getting a divorce from an absolute horror, and she didn't want Benedict's name connected with hers until she was free. All I knew was that she was seeing "the most wonderful man in the world", and they were crazily in love. It was only when I went to see her last week, and the nurse said her only male caller had been the great Mr Peters, that I twigged it and tackled Barbie, and she admitted it.'

'Benedict Peters,' muttered Colin. 'Who'd have believed it? It's pretty lousy behaviour, I agree, but—well, maybe he stopped loving her.'

'From one day to the next?' Sara snorted.

'What does Barbie say about it?'

'She still defends him, can you believe! Says they mutually agreed to call things off.'

'Maybe it's true.'

'Even if it was—which I'm sure it wasn't—couldn't he have had the decency to have waited till she was home again—or at least well on the mend?'

'I can't argue against that,' Colin conceded. 'But . . . well, none of this concerns you, and I still can't see why you shouldn't audition for him.'

'Because I'm an opera singer, and I'm not about to throw away my training.'

'You're throwing it away just by staying here! Come back to my place and listen to the tape the director sent me.

It might make you change your mind.'

'It won't,' Sara said. 'Though I'd like to hear it anyway.' A thought struck her. 'How come they sent you a tape, though? If you're only auditioning for the chorus . . .'

'I'm not.' Colin tried to look modest and failed. 'I'm up for the second male lead. Some of the songs have a wide vocal range and Peters is looking for someone with operatic training.'

Sara appreciated why as she listened to the music some half an hour later. It was brilliant. Yet instead of this softening her attitude to its composer, she despised him for wasting his talent on ephemeral nonsense.

'His three other musicals weren't nonsense,' Colin protested when she aired her views. 'They both ran for years and were smash hits as films.'

'He's been lucky,' Sara shrugged.

'Which is why you should be in his new show. At least you'd be eating for years to come!'

She laughed and shook her head, and Colin switched off the tape deck. His profile was turned towards her, and the angle made him look younger than twenty-seven. Dear Colin! She'd miss him terribly when he left the company, but from his point of view he was doing the right thing. Not just musically, but emotionally—for he'd been in love with her for years, and though she kept telling him he was wasting his time, he still harboured hopes of making her change her mind.

'Take the cassette and listen to it again,' he urged, drawing her close. 'Then if you want to audition, give me a call and I'll arrange it.'

She nodded and tried to pull away from him, but he lowered his head and began kissing her. As the pressure of his mouth increased and he tried to force her lips apart, she could not bear the intimacy and pushed him away.

'Why do you keep fighting me?' he asked huskily. 'I want to marry you, Sara.'

'I don't love you,' she said, keeping her voice light. 'Except as a sister!'

'Well, until there's another man in your life I've no intention of acting your brother! You can't remain single for ever just because of your lousy experience with Martin.'

She grimaced ruefully. How positive she had been that Martin had meant his promise to marry her; and how bitter the shock when he'd ditched her for an older, sophisticated divorcee.

'It's five years since you've seen him,' Colin went on. 'You can't still care for him.'

'I don't,' she stated truthfully. 'But he's made me wary of men.'

'You mean you don't trust me either?'

'I'd trust you with my life, Colin, but I don't love you.'

He knew better than to argue with her, though his stubborn expression showed he wasn't going to change his mind. She only hoped that once he was in London and away from her, he would meet someone else.

The following week he left the company, and five days later jubilantly wrote he had landed the part he wanted in *Girl In A Million*.

'They're still looking for someone to sing Daisy, the character who'll be playing opposite me,' he concluded, 'and you could do it like a dream.'

But Sara wouldn't be persuaded, and wrote back assuring him she was perfectly happy where she was. They were fine words that she was forced to eat a month later, when the company closed and she found herself jobless.

'I've nothing suitable for you on my books,' her agent said when she returned to London, a week's salary in her purse. 'You'll either have to broaden your horizon, or resign yourself to resting.'

John Levine leaned back in his leather chair and moved his cigar from one side of his mouth to the other. 'If I tried to pull the wool over your eyes I'd be a lousy agent.'

'You're a great agent,' she said. 'So what can you offer if I *do* broaden my horizon?'

'The chance of getting you on to a TV show called *New Talent*.'

'Oh no, I couldn't!' she protested.

'Why not? It would do wonders for your career if you won. Choose a really popular number and you'll be in there with a great chance.'

'Something like "Ave Maria" or "One Fine Day"?' she asked drily.

'What's wrong with a fine day?' He wrote a name on a slip of paper and handed it to her. 'Go see Bob Jackson. He's the producer.'

'What's the prize if I win?'

'Be lucky first and get chosen to enter!' John picked up the phone. 'I'll fix your appointment for tomorrow morning. Be at London TV at ten-thirty, and make yourself beautiful.'

'Don't I always?'

'What I meant was sexy. Use more make-up and wear something that clings!'

Sara nodded, though she had no intention of taking his advice. To assume a persona that wasn't hers would make her so uncomfortable she'd give a rotten performance. Far better to look herself and trust her voice was good enough to do the trick.

It was a somewhat abashed Sara who telephoned Colin later in the day to tell him she was in London and auditioning for *New Talent*. To his credit he didn't say 'I told you so', merely that he was delighted to have her near him again, and when could they meet.

'Any time after tomorrow,' she said. 'I want to spend tonight resting my voice.'

She was unusually nervous when she presented herself at London TV's studio in Harlesden next morning, and was shown into a large, bare rehearsal room.

Some dozen contestants were ahead of her, and about the same number of eager-faced hopefuls behind. As she looked at the various juggling acts, ventriloquists and guitarists, her heart sank. But once she had given her music to the pianist and was ready to sing, her nervousness vanished. She had a good voice and knew how to use it. Too bad for the producer if he didn't recognise it!

The pianist played the opening chord of 'One Fine Day', and Sara went into it effortlessly, unaware how lovely she looked in her simple cream-coloured suit, her amber hair falling straight and soft to her shoulders.

She looked as delicate as a Watteau shepherdess, her skin tinged pink by the single spotlight a zealous electrician had directed on her, its brilliance finding no flaw in her heart-shaped face, straight nose and small, full mouth. As a child she had often been cast as an angel in the Nativity play, until maturity had highlighted the provocative allure of slanting green eyes masked at will by absurdly long lashes.

As she came to the end of the aria there was a hushed silence. Then several people clapped, and Sara blushingly walked over to the producer.

'That was great, Miss James. I'll book you on our show six weeks from now.' He saw her dismay. 'Can't you make it then?'

'Oh yes. It's just that I was hoping it would be sooner.'

''Fraid not. We're booked solid.' He smiled down at her. 'Have a word with Tony Phillips, our musical director. He'll advise you about your song.'

Tony Phillips—a puckish man in his early forties—was more than willing to oblige, saying he'd heard her audition and loved her voice.

'But you should key your act to your audience,' he advised, 'and ours is a fairly lowbrow one. You'd shorten the odds considerably in your favour if you chose something more modern.'

'I'll do anything you say,' she told him.

'That's half the battle, then! I'm off on vacation tomorrow, but call me in three weeks and we can arrange a date for you to come and rehearse with me.'

Pleased at the way things were going, Sara returned to her bedsit. She was curious to discover what song he would pick for her, and knew she'd be willing to sing 'My Old Man's a Dustman' if it would win her first prize. The only song she wouldn't touch with a bargepole was anything written by Benedict Peters.

No sooner had Sara stepped into her room than Colin rang to see how her audition had gone. He was delighted to hear she had been accepted, and stunned to learn that Tony Phillips was going to coach her.

'If *he* can't turn you into a winner, no one can. I hope you'll remember me when you're famous!'

'If I don't die of starvation first! I've got six weeks to wait till I go on the show.'

'They're still auditioning for the chorus for *this* one.'

'Where do I go?' Sara capitulated.

'Round the corner from London TV! I'll collect you in the morning.'

Promptly at nine, he called for her in a smart little Fiat.

'Yours?' she asked, climbing in.

'By courtesy of Benedict Peters. His name's as good as a letter from the bank manager!' Colin gave her a quick glance as he pulled out into the stream of traffic. 'You're looking very lovely, Sara. I've missed you.'

She let the comment pass, knowing any conversation she and Colin had would inevitably centre on herself, and was glad when they arrived at the church hall where rehearsals were taking place.

It was bare and cold despite several large electric fans belching out hot air. Though it was nothing to the hot air exuded by the dancers and singers milling around waiting for their casting call.

'Which queue do I join?' asked Sara.

'None. You've someone of influence beside you, darling!'

Hand under her elbow, Colin guided her to where a bone-thin man in his forties was sitting astride a chair, listening to a well-developed young woman with an under-developed voice screech out the first few bars of a Peters number.

'Thank you,' the man said, stopping her in mid-shriek. 'Your voice isn't what we're looking for right now. Sorry.'

As the girl walked away, Colin pushed Sara forward. 'Mr Kelly, this is the girl I was telling you about.'

'The undiscovered Callas!' grunted Tom Kelly, eyeing her. 'OK, give me the opening number.'

Dismayed, Sara glanced at Colin. Why hadn't he warned her to come prepared?

'It's "Midnight Blues",' he hissed in her ear, picking up a music sheet from a pile on the top of the piano and thrusting it into her hand.

Casting a quick eye over it, Sara launched into the refrain without waiting for the pianist, and had barely sung a verse when the chorus-master stopped her.

'OK,' he called. 'You're in!'

Knowing she would at least be eating properly from now on, Sara gave him her agent's name, and in return was given the theatrical costumiers, where she had to go to be measured for her costumes.

To her surprise she thoroughly enjoyed working in the musical, the more so as there was no sign of Benedict Peters, who was in New York putting the finishing touches to the Broadway version that would be opening some months after the British one.

The two lead singers weren't joining the cast until a month before the opening, and meanwhile understudies filled in for them. Occasionally it seemed to Sara that the singers worked far harder than the dancers, but in reality this was untrue, for every member of the cast was important to the show's success.

The atmosphere was far more easygoing than with an opera company, with everyone on Christian-name terms and a great deal of familiarity among the less important members of the cast. Colin was in his element in this uninhibited atmosphere, and she was amused by the way Ella Brown, who played his girlfriend Daisy, was as warmly responsive to him off stage as on.

Unfortunately he paid her no attention, and Sara decided that if she didn't get anywhere with the *New Talent* contest, she'd join an opera company abroad and put herself completely out of his orbit.

Surprisingly, the thought of leaving the musical depressed her, for she found it absorbing to watch it take shape and form.

'I told you it would get to you,' said Colin, delighted by her changed feelings. 'This could well be the smash hit of the eighties!'

'The songs are good enough,' she agreed, and wished she could divorce Benedict Peters' talent from his outrageous behaviour to her friend. After all, one thing had nothing to do with the other.

Yet the mere mention of his name brought Barbie to mind, and she wondered how anyone who could compose such heart-catching music and lyrics could walk out on a girl when she was at her lowest ebb.

Three weeks slowly passed, and on the morning of the fourth Monday, Sara rang London TV to speak to Tony Phillips.

'I'm afraid I can't see you during the day,' she apologised. 'I'm in the chorus of the new Benedict Peters show.'

'Then we'll make it an evening. Come round to my home in Fulham—Oak Tree Lane, last house on the left. Is eight o'clock tonight OK?'

She hesitated. She barely knew the man and was in no mood for a sexual hassle. Yet if she refused to see him . . .

'I'm not going to pounce on you,' he grunted. 'You'll

know why when you meet my wife!'

Agreeing to see him at eight, Sara returned to the rehearsal hall.

She had only been away a few minutes, but the instant she walked in she sensed a change in the atmosphere: there was an alertness, a sense of tension in it. The dancers were limbering up; the male half of the chorus were rehearsing one song on stage, while the female half sang another at the opposite end of the hall; the dress designer was frantically unravelling bolts of material in the far corner, while the scenic designer looked at them with brooding eyes and scribbled notes on his pad.

But everyone was surreptitiously eyeing the two men sitting near the piano, though Sara only recognised the grey head of the director, Merrit Clay.

'OK, Betty,' he called to the choreographer. 'Show us the next routine—from the eighth bar.'

'I'd like B.P. to see it from the beginning,' the choreographer panted, her leotard sweat-stained.

'Another time, Betty,' an incisive male voice interpolated. 'If you're handling it, I know I've nothing to worry about. In fact I'll wait and see the whole routine later. Meanwhile, take a break.'

The choreographer looked pleased, though the dancers ambled off stage like dispirited swans.

Sara clutched at Colin's arm. 'I didn't know Benedict Peters was back!'

'He flew in last night.'

Covertly she glanced at the man beside Merrit. He had risen and was walking their way, still talking in low tones to the director. He was quite different from what she had imagined, or from how Barbie had described him the first time she had written about him to Sara. He was taller and darker for a start, and older too. But then Barbie had a tendency to see people as she'd like them to be, rather than as they were. Hence her disastrous marriage!

The composer stopped a few yards away from them and was joined by the choreographer, whose flirtatious manner gave the lie to rumours that she did not like men. Yet one would have to be very anti-men not to appreciate this one, for he was fairytale good-looking, with straight, firm features, thick black hair and a six-foot frame that would have done justice to a rugger player.

And did he know it! Despite his seeming indifference to the female glances cast in his direction, there was arrogance in the tilt of his head, assuredness in his determined stance, and a devil-may-care nonchalance in the faintly cynical smile that curved his wide mouth.

Poor Barbie. How could she ever have hoped to hold the attention of such a man? Sara thought sadly. Darling though she was, she was so gentle she'd have ended up his doormat.

Her mind absorbed by these thoughts, she looked in his direction and saw him staring at her. Close to, she was aware that his nose flared slightly at the nostrils, its patrician cast mediated by the shapely curve of his mouth. But it was his eyes that drew her. Deep-set beneath strongly marked brows—and grey-green like her own—they were regarding her with compelling intensity, and Sara, knowing it would serve little purpose to show her animosity, averted her head.

'Will the chorus go into the opening number,' Merrit ordered. 'And would the baritones come in sharp on the sixth bar for a change and surprise me!'

Everyone rushed for the stage, Sara among them, and the rousing song that opened the show was belted out the way it had been rehearsed. Sara's voice soared effortlessly, all else forgotten except her joy in the music, and the song finished on a crescendo that drowned out the piano.

There was a short silence before Benedict Peters spoke.

'Thank you, ladies and gentlemen. That was an excellent rendition, though unfortunately not the one I want!'

'Too much enthusiasm,' Merrit put in.

'Too much voice, actually,' Benedict Peters corrected. 'Will the Joan Sutherland in the back row please step forward?'

Nobody moved, and it took a few seconds and some backward glances from the front line of the chorus before Sara realised he meant her! Blushing profusely, she pushed her way through to the front.

'The essence of a chorus,' he said pleasantly, 'is to emit a simultaneous musical sound. It's not a contest. If it were, you'd undoubtedly reign supreme.'

'I wasn't trying to be supreme, Mr Peters,' she replied. 'I was singing as I always do.'

'Well, it won't do here.' He turned to Merrit. 'This song heralds Magda's first appearance. *She's* the main character, for God's sake, so put a cover over the cage of this twittering canary!'

Green eyes blazing, Sara advanced to the edge of the stage. 'There's no need for you to be so bloody rude!'

'I'm sorry you object to my bluntness.'

'Rudeness, I said, Mr Peters, not bluntness! And don't bother covering the cage, because this is one canary that won't trill for you!'

Buoyed by anger, Sara stalked from the hall, and was in the lobby when Colin caught up with her, his face flushed with distress.

'You shouldn't take any notice of Peters,' he told her, 'I'm told he's often bad-tempered at rehearsals. But he doesn't mean it.'

'Yes, he does!' she said furiously.

'Maybe he did come on a bit strong,' Colin agreed. 'But he wasn't wrong, you know. You *were* singing above everybody else.'

'Which proves I'm not cut out for this sort of music.' She pulled free of his restraining hand. 'I'm leaving, Colin.'

'What will you do instead?'

'Take a job as a daily, or do waitressing. I can find loads of things to tide me over till the television show. After that, if I win . . .'

'Say you don't?'

'Then it's back to opera.'

'You're cutting off your nose to spite your face,' he warned.

'It's my face,' Sara shrugged.

'OK, if that's how you feel . . .' He gave her arm a squeeze. 'Have supper with me tonight?'

'I'm rehearsing at Tony's.'

'I'll meet you outside afterwards.'

Back in her bedsit, Sara was far less complacent about her future than she had sounded. Nor was she sure that opera could again become the focus of her existence. As Tony rightly said, there were many different branches of music, and if she had difficulty succeeding in one, it was foolish not to try another. So far she'd got nowhere in opera or musicals, and if she failed in the talent show, she'd have to rethink her career.

She gave a bitter laugh. Pity she hadn't followed her mother's advice and become a secretary. At least she would never have met the rudest man in the world. 'Twittering canary' indeed!

CHAPTER TWO

THERE were two good things about leaving the musical: Sara no longer felt guilty each time she saw Barbie—she had never told her friend she was singing in the show, and now, thank goodness, there was no need to do so—and she had plenty of time to rehearse with Tony Phillips.

He was the hardest taskmaster she had had, and the hours spent in his studio on the top floor of his Edwardian house were a combination of pleasure and misery. Pleasure when she sang the way he wanted, misery when she forgot and sang like an operatic diva!

'In opera, the voice matters above everything else,' he had said. 'But with pop music, the way you deliver the lyrics is equally important.'

'I don't think I have the aptitude for these kind of songs,' she had sighed despondently.

'Don't give me that! All you need is the right coaching—which is why you're here.'

'You really think I can win the contest?'

'No question of it! I'd back you against a juggler any day! All you have to do is listen to the good singers in this field, Sara. Study how they interpret a song, then dig down inside yourself to find *your* style.'

'Not easy,' she had muttered.

'Who told you success comes easily? You have to sweat at it.'

And sweat she did, working as a waitress during the day, rehearsing with Tony most evenings, and listening to tapes at the weekends.

The evening before her television appearance, Tony and his wife Anna—a statuesque brunette half a head taller than her husband—took her to dinner at Tante Claire, one of London's gourmet restaurants.

'Maybe we should have waited till tomorrow before coming here,' Sara murmured, looking round the discreetly opulent room where they were sitting.

'From tomorrow night you'll be walking two feet off the ground,' teased Anna. 'Besides, it's now—when you're nervous—that you need an ego-booster.'

Tante Claire was certainly that, and by the time their delicious meal was at an end Sara, replete with magnificent French cuisine and wine, could think of the contest without a qualm.

But her fear returned with full force as she entered the make-up room at the television studio, and she prayed she wouldn't let Tony down. Realising that if the judges' decision was a close one, her appearance could well swing the vote in her favour, she had pawned her gold watch to buy the most expensive dress she had ever owned: a sea-green silk whose colour almost exactly matched her eyes. The material curved subtly round her body, making her look incredibly fine-boned and fragile, almost too fragile to house such a strong, resonant voice.

'You're the best-looking contestant we've had in months,' the make-up girl told her, eyeing her critically. 'And you've applied the warpaint pretty well too! All you need is a touch of shadow along your jawline.'

'I'm used to getting made up,' Sara grinned. 'I'm in show business.'

'I guessed it.' The girl dabbed a brush around Sara's chin. 'You're so calm and confident.'

On the outside only, Sara thought a little later as the producer's secretary led her across to the side of the stage.

The first act—a comedian—was already performing, and the audience's laughter showed he was doing well. The next act, an impressionist, did even better, and nervous though she was, Sara couldn't help laughing at his brilliant impersonations.

'You look perfect,' said Tony beside her, and she swung round to see him appraising her dress and hair. She had piled it on top of her head, allowing tendrils to escape and curl about her ears and along the sides of her neck.

'Perfect,' he repeated. 'Stay cool and you'll romp home.'

'I'm scared witless!' she confessed.

She clutched his arm as the sound of clapping signified that she was the next one on, and her legs trembled so much she couldn't move. Tony gave her a none too gentle shove in the direction of the compère, who grasped her elbow and led her on stage.

From the moment Sara launched into her ballad, she sensed she held the audience in the palm of her hand, and she was proved right when the final note died away and the auditorium erupted with a storm of applause.

Blinking away happy tears, she glanced towards the wings where Tony was grinning like a Cheshire Cat. Shakily she returned to him. She had been the last to perform, and now her future lay with the judges.

'You were marvellous,' Tony beamed. 'Benedict Peters will never hear that sung better!'

'You mean he's in the audience?' Sara trembled at the knowledge. Thank heavens she hadn't known beforehand!

'More than that, sweetheart. He's one of the judges. If he doesn't ask you to be his next leading lady, I'll eat my hat!'

'I'm afraid you'll have to,' she said shakily. 'You know very well he's no admirer of mine.'

'He's a professional, and that's how he'll judge you. If he——'

The rest of what he said was drowned by a roll of drums as the compère stepped forward to announce the winners.

Sara's heart was beating so loudly she could hear nothing else, but the look on Tony's face told her all she needed to know, and shaking like a leaf in a storm, she walked back on stage to meet the judges.

As she reached Benedict Peters she forced herself to look at him. God, he was handsome! And he knew it too, as he sauntered towards her, his black dinner jacket no darker than his glossy hair, a white silk sweater—instead of the normal dress shirt—giving him a slumbrous, sensual look.

'A well-deserved win,' he murmured.

'Thank you.'

With a tight smile she turned to the second judge who, it seemed, ran a chain of theatres up North, and was ready to book her into every one of them!

'She'll be too busy with me.' This from Dick Cawthorne, the third judge and owner of Cawthorne Records. 'When can we talk business, Miss James?'

'You'll have to speak to my agent, John Levine,' she told him.

'I'll do that.'

Several more people spoke to her, but she was too dazed to take in what they said, and was relieved when Tony rescued her by saying the producer was giving a party in the hospitality room, and it couldn't start without her.

'Don't put your signature to anything,' he warned when they were alone in the elevator. 'Apart from Peters, they're a load of sharks.'

'And he isn't?' she enquired drily.

'When it comes to business there's no nicer guy. You should try to persuade him to write some numbers for you.'

'After the way we parted, the only thing he'd write is a dirge for my funeral!'

'Don't exaggerate. Anyway, you can always say you're sorry.'

'But I'm not!'

Before Tony could comment, they reached the hospitality room, where everyone connected with the show was being entertained.

Colin came hurrying over and gave Sara an exuberant

kiss. 'You're a star!' he exclaimed.

A glass of wine was thrust into her hand and a toast was drunk. People crowded round to congratulate her, and there was a great deal of laughter and frothy conversation.

She was on her second glass and feeling rather high when, turning to reach for a slice of quiche, she found her way barred by the one man she didn't want to see!

'I've been waiting my chance to talk to you,' said Benedict Peters. 'You sang that ballad exactly the way I've always wanted to hear it, Miss James. You've a lovely voice.'

'Really?' Her tone was icy. 'You change your mind quickly.'

Grey-green eyes regarded her with puzzlement. 'I don't follow you.'

Sara glared at him. He was either a consummate actor or had completely forgotten their last encounter. She rather suspected it was the latter, which did nothing to improve her temper. To know he didn't remember his insult was an even bigger insult!

'Why do you dislike me so much?' he went on softly, and as she still did not answer, he added, 'Are you implying that I've heard you sing before?'

'Exactly,' she cooed in her sweetest tone. 'Though perhaps you prefer to blot out the memory. After all, it can't be pleasant to have a twittering canary reverberating in your ears!'

'A twittering . . .?' Perplexity gave way to amusement, lightening his eyes and giving them a silvery sparkle. 'The girl in the chorus who thought she was Joan Sutherland? Well, I'll be damned!'

'I'm sure you *have* been,' Sara replied. 'They say the devil always looks after his own—which probably accounts for your success!'

Her retort, so promptly spoken, startled him, making her realise how vitriolic she had been. Not that she would take back a word of it. A man like him deserved far worse.

'You've a vicious tongue, Miss James,' he said quietly. 'But you're using a hammer to kill a gnat.'

It was on the tip of her tongue to tell him it was more because of Barbie, rather than his insulting comment about her voice, that made her dislike him, when she decided not to. He was so used to women falling down like ninepins when he so much as looked at them that it would be a bigger blow to his ego for him to believe he'd finally encountered one who was immune to him.

'Now you've jogged my memory about our last meeting,' he continued, 'your success tonight merely proves how right I was. Your voice is far too good to fit into a chorus!'

'You can say that again!' interpolated Tony, joining them in time to hear the last sentence. 'I hope you'll remember Sara next time you're casting!'

'I'm not likely to forget her,' Benedict Peters replied, and with a mocking salute, moved away.

'Hateful man,' she muttered. 'I wouldn't work for him if it was the last job on earth.'

'I hope you don't mean that. If you aren't willing to do what's best for your career, get out of the business.'

Sara was mulling this over when Colin rejoined them. He was still beaming with delight at her success, and she warmed to him. How kind he was, with no hidden depths and no great inquisitiveness of mind. Some girl would be lucky to have him as a husband. But not her. There'd be no heights of ecstasy for her if she married him, and though there wouldn't be any troughs of despair either, she was too young to settle for second best.

Over his shoulder she glimpsed a haughty profile beneath curling black hair. So the great composer was still honouring the party with his presence! Deliberately she linked her arm through Colin's and gave him a warm smile.

'I'll leave you two lovebirds alone,' Tony said diplomatically, and wandered off.

'If only it were true,' whispered Colin, bending his head to bring his mouth close to Sara's ear. 'I was so proud of you tonight, I wanted to stand up and shout that you were mine.'

'Like a doll you long to own?' she teased.

'No one could ever own you, Sara. You're too independent. But if you could love me a little . . .'

She withdrew her arm from his, regretting the impulse that had prompted her to take hold of it. What was she trying to prove anyway? That she had a boyfriend and didn't need Benedict Peters? The whole thing was crazy.

'I wish you'd accept the way I feel about you, Colin, and stop pushing me,' she told him. 'If you don't, I'll stop seeing you.'

'Then I have no choice, have I?' Colin drew her hand to his lips. 'I'm not letting you out of my life!'

Sara bit back a sigh. His devotion made her realise how empty her future would be without love. Family and friends had their own special niche, but without one special man with whom to share her success, it was all going to be very futile.

Angrily she pushed the thought away. What a time to be thinking like this—when success seemed hers for the asking! She must reach for it, utilise it, hold on to it for all it was worth. She might never become another Callas—as she had dreamed when first embarking on her career—but at least she'd be singing and getting paid for it!

CHAPTER THREE

THE FOLLOWING morning John Levine rang Sara to say Dick Cawthorne was prepared to offer her a recording contract.

'So goodbye opera,' she sighed.

'Not necessarily. Once you're famous, you can sing where you like.'

'Including the Met and Covent Garden?' she questioned. 'Don't kid me, John.'

'I'm not. Nothing succeeds like success, and when you're in the big league you'll be able to move any way you like.'

Sara considered his remark. He had never tried to influence her in order to earn himself a commission, and she would be foolish to ignore his advice.

'Very well,' she conceded. 'Set up a meeting for me with Mr Cawthorne.'

'I have,' he boomed jovially. 'My office, ten-thirty Monday. Enjoy your weekend!'

Smiling, she returned to the kitchen to finish her breakfast and read the morning paper, delighted that one of the most influential TV critics had described her as 'the new nightingale on the pop scene'.

'If I were Benedict Peters,' he concluded, 'I'd let no one but Miss James touch my songs.'

Mr Peters eat your heart out! Sara thought, and remembering her mortification that he had forgotten their first meeting, hoped he had read this review.

The next few hours were spent answering congratulatory calls until finally, in desperation, she switched on her answerphone and settled down to clean the kitchenette and bedroom. Glimpsing her apron-clad figure in a mirror, she grinned. If only her fans could see her now!

At one o'clock, refreshed after a cool shower, she listened to her messages: more friends congratulating her, Colin inviting her to dinner—she had no intention of accepting—and Barbie to say how thrilled she was by Sara's success the previous night.

Guilt at having neglected her friend these past hectic weeks decided Sara to spend the rest of the day with her, and early that afternoon she arrived at Barbie's garden flat—euphemism for basement—armed with two fillet steaks and a bottle of champagne.

'What a marvellous surprise!' Barbie greeted her, limping into the kitchen to put the meat into the refrigerator. 'I thought you'd be lunching at the Connaught surrounded by admirers!'

'All drinking champagne from my slipper?' Sara mocked. 'Which reminds me, I'm dying for a coffee!' With the familiarity of long friendship she filled the percolator and switched it on.

'You were wonderful last night,' Barbie enthused. 'You sang Benedict's song fantastically.'

'Maybe. But I loathed every note. Just the thought of him makes me so mad I could spit!'

'That's crazy talk! What happened between him and me has nothing to do with you.'

'I know, but——'

'You can't condemn him for changing his mind,' Barbie insisted.

'I condemn him for ditching you when you needed him most. I'm amazed you can even speak his name without puking!' Barbie lowered her head and said nothing, and Sara sighed. 'Turning from one skunk to another, what's happening with Alec and your divorce?'

'The date's been set for the hearing, thank goodness.'

Barbie's tone was matter-of-fact, but colour had flooded her face, making Sara think how pretty she would be if she were a few pounds heavier. In the past they had often been taken for sisters; Barbie a darker version perhaps, with brown eyes instead of green, and hair more beige than amber. But they were both slender and graceful, though at the moment Barbie had a limp and was skin and bone, obviously pining for Benedict, regardless of what she said.

'Alec came here one night to see me,' Barbie broke into Sara's thoughts, 'but I wouldn't let him in.'

'I should think not!' Remembering the gregarious engineer who had swept Barbie off her feet five years ago, and then driven her to despair with his womanising, Sara was astonished he had the audacity to show his face.

'You wouldn't go back to him, would you?' she questioned, knowing how vulnerable one could be on the rebound.

'Never! I'd rather be alone the rest of my life.'

Hoping Mr Marvellous will return to her, Sara thought sourly, and was curious to know where the two of them had met. On the face of it, they were worlds apart. Benedict's was show business, with all its attendant excitement, while Barbie's . . . Sara glanced through the window at the small patio crowded with gaily coloured pots which her friend filled with bouquets of flowers which she dried herself, and sold to gift shops.

'How did you meet the great composer?' she asked, deciding that as they'd been talking about him, she might as well satisfy her curiosity.

'In my doctor's waiting room.'

Sara's beautifully arched eyebrows lifted, unable to picture him in a general practitioner's surgery off the Fulham Road. A Harley Street specialist was more his line!

'The doctor was his cousin,' Barbie explained.

'The only men I ever meet at my doctor's are old-age pensioners!' Sara said lightly.

Barbie laughed and poured the coffee, then carried the mugs into the sitting room. 'What's happening between you and Colin?' she asked.

'Nothing. If I——'

The peal of the telephone sent Barbie rushing to answer it. But seeing the anticipation leave her face, Sara knew it was not the call she had expected. She was definitely hoping to hear from that bloody man! It was all Sara could do to keep quiet, but she had already said enough, and she reminded herself that a friend was not a keeper.

'Why don't you go home for a few weeks?' she suggested. 'You look as if you could do with some country air.'

'I'd be too restless, with the divorce hanging over me.'

'Are you expecting trouble from Alec?'

'He's always trouble,' sighed Barbie.

'Was that why Benedict walked out on you? Because he was scared of what Alec might do?'

'Certainly not,' Barbie retorted, though the colour that swept into her face denied what she said. 'I was the one who was scared of that, which is why I kept our relationship secret, and why I still don't want anyone to know about it.'

'I only mentioned it to Colin,' Sara assured her, 'and he'll be silent as the grave. Which reminds me,' she added, determined to change the subject, 'my mother grieves for Dad as much *now* as she did five years ago.'

'That's terrible!'

'I know. I'm sure it's because she's stayed on in the same house and taken care of the doctor who bought Dad's practice. I begged her to move to another town and build a new life for herself, but she wouldn't.'

'Can't she stay with you now?' Barbie suggested. 'As a famous star, you can't go on living in a bedsit!'

'You've got a point there,' Sara chuckled. 'And it's a jolly good way of forcing my mother's hand. I'll think I'll say it's important for me to have a glamorous lifestyle and that I need her to manage my private affairs.'

'You probably will,' stated Barbie. 'Your days of anonymity are over. I feel it in my bones.'

So did Sara, especially when she met Dick Cawthorne in John's office. The two men couldn't have looked more unalike. John, big and bluff in tweeds, seemingly ready for a day at the races; Dick Cawthorne, neat-featured, with grey-flecked hair, looking more like a banker than a record producer.

She was astounded by the amount he was willing to invest in her, and amazed that a large portion of it would go on creating a new image for her.

'I get the impression you're buying the voice box and throwing out the rest!' she couldn't help saying.

'In a way I am. And I hope you'll trust my judgement.' He leaned back in his chair, relaxed and urbane. 'I manage some of the biggest names in this business, and not one of them has left me for another recording company. I think that speaks for itself.'

It certainly did, and though Sara had reservations about her new career, she intuitively knew this man was the best one to handle it.

'If you're willing to back me, Mr Cawthorne,' she said, 'I'm willing to work my butt off!'

In the weeks that followed, Sara did.

To her delight, Dick asked Tony Phillips to be her musical director, making him responsible for choosing her songs and orchestrating them.

A nightclub tour was booked for her—'It's the best way of learning how to handle an audience,' Dick assured her— and seeing Newcastle, Manchester and Birmingham on the list, she ruefully acknowledged that she might as well have remained with the opera company! Except that the money spent promoting her was more than her old company had earned in a year!

Dick had also meant what he said about giving her a new image. A hairdresser flew from Paris to restyle her hair, cutting it slightly shorter so that it swung more freely as she moved her head, and tipping the ends with silver, which immediately gave her a sharper image that went well with the strong, clear colours of her new clothes—designed for her by Karl Lagerfeld, a name she had, till now, seen only in *Vogue*.

One of Estée Lauder's leading make-up men worked on her face like an artist on a canvas, and Sara—who considered herself pretty but not eye-catching—was astonished by the difference he made to her. She had never realised she had the high cheekbones and slanting eyes of Sophia Loren, coupled with the fragile allure of a young Audrey Hepburn!

Dick was as delighted with her appearance as she was, and three weeks after their meeting in John's office, he invited her to dinner at the St James Club.

Its quiet, elegant atmosphere suited him well, and her initial awe of him disappeared as she discovered him to be an intelligent companion whose horizons extended beyond his own profession. After a brief reference to her forthcoming nightclub tour, they spent the meal talking ecology and politics.

'You're a knowledgeable young woman,' he commented over coffee. 'Most girls of your age are just pretty faces.'

'That's what most men prefer!'

'True, I'm afraid. I did too, when I was young. But now I've learned more sense!'

The rasp in his voice told her his experience hadn't come painlessly, and his next words confirmed it.

'I married a dumb blonde at thirty, stuck it out till I was forty, and have been happily divorced ever since—which is enabling me to spend my fiftieth birthday with a beautiful young singer who's going to be one of my greatest successes—professionally speaking, of course!'

'Your birthday?' Sara exclaimed. 'I'd have bought you a present if I'd known.'

'I'm too old for presents.'

'Nonsense! My parents were always giving each other things. Nothing expensive, just silly little tokens.'

'Sounds like you come from a happy home.'

'I did,' she sighed. 'But it fell apart when my father died. Mother tried to keep things going as they'd always been, but it wasn't easy. I'm hoping she'll come and live with me now I can afford a bigger place.'

'If you're looking for somewhere, I may be able to help you,' Dick said. 'I own several apartment blocks, and one of them still has a few vacancies. I'll be happy to let you buy one at cost.'

Sara was annoyed to find herself blushing. Dick's offer was generous, but she wasn't naïve enough to take it at face value.

'You're doing us both an injustice,' he commented drily. 'You're a lovely young woman, Sara, but I'm no believer in the lasting quality of a May-to-December relationship! I assure you my offer has no strings attached.'

'I'm glad,' she smiled, then realising her comment was two-edged, looked so dismayed that he laughed.

'Think of me as a family friend,' he said, writing an address on one of his cards and handing it to her. 'I'll be controlling a major portion of your life and it's important that we're at ease with each other.'

Arms on the table, he regarded her with shrewd brown eyes. 'John mentioned that your boy friend's in Benedict's new musical,' he observed.

'The accent's on "friend",' she stated. 'We aren't lovers.'

'Speaking of lovers,' Dick murmured, glancing across her shoulder, 'said composer's just walked in with Carol Dean—an ex-flame of his.'

'Is that how she got the lead in his new show?'

'I doubt it. B. P.'s too tough a nut to let the sensual rule his sense! She got the part because she's good.'

Colin had said the same, for the American singer had arrived a few days ago, and the cast were now rehearsing in the West End theatre where they were due to open in a month.

'She's a professional to her fingertips,' he had told Sara. 'Right now she's at the honeymoon stage with the company, but I've heard she can be a real bitch if she's not continually in the limelight.'

'Like most stars,' Sara had countered. 'People may say the same about us one day!'

'Let me only be a star!' Colin had replied, rolling his eyes.

'How well do you know her?' Sara asked Dick now.

'Only by repute. But that's going to be remedied in about ten seconds—they're coming over to us!'

He stood up as he spoke, and the hair on Sara's head prickled as Benedict Peters came into her line of vision and stopped at their table.

'Hello, Dick,' he said. 'I just wanted to congratulate you on Sage and Onions' new album. I think you're on to a winner.'

'Coming from you that's a real compliment,' the older man smiled. 'But my biggest win is sitting right here.' He indicated Sara.

Benedict's mouth lifted in a smile that did not reach his eyes. 'How are you enjoying your new life, Miss James?' he asked her.

'I'm too busy to know.' Sara avoided looking at him by the simple expedient of focusing on the girl beside him, and with a slightly mocking bow, he made the introductions.

Carol Dean favoured her and Dick with a scarlet-lipped smile that disclosed perfect teeth. Her eyes were bright and black as a magpie's, as was the colour of her short, curly hair. Exceptionally tall—her head was on a level with Benedict's chin—she was slim as a reed except for voluptuous breasts which, though concealed beneath one of St Laurent's 'little black dresses', clearly required no bra to keep them firmly uptilted.

'How long are you booked for the London show?' Dick asked her.

'Until the Broadway one opens.'

'We really need two Carols,' Benedict asserted. 'One here and one in New York!'

'There's only one Carol Dean,' said Dick gallantly.

'And right now she's starving to death!' the girl grinned, slipping a hand through Benedict's arm.

'Upon which hint I'll go feed the lady,' he said. 'See you at the first night, Dick.' His eyes flicked to Sara. 'If you'd like a couple of tickets, Miss James . . .'

'Colin's already given me two.'

'Ah yes, I'd forgotten you know Colin.'

He and Carol moved off, and Dick sat down. 'I'm glad we bumped into him tonight,' he said. 'I'd like him to write for you.'

'I wouldn't.'

'Why?'

Wishing Barbie hadn't sworn her to secrecy, Sara gave Dick the 'canary' episode as her reason.

'I can see why it infuriated you,' he chuckled, 'but forget it and think of your career. He can give it a big lift.'

It was a statement she couldn't deny, and she sighed acceptance of it.

Glad of his victory, Dick changed the subject, but Sara was still unnervingly conscious of Benedict's presence, and though she couldn't see his table, his image was engraved in her mind's eye. There was no denying he was a macho man, and she could picture the tall leanness of him, the raw sensuality, the faintly sardonic expression in his hooded eyes.

Why kid herself? If it hadn't been for Barbie, she could have fallen for him hook, line and sinker! And would probably have been ditched like the rest of his girlfriends too!

'You seem restless,' Dick commented. 'Does B.P.'s

presence worry you so much?'

'Not at all,' she lied. 'I'm just tired. Tony's a hard taskmaster.'

'Then I'll take you home.'

'I'm not that tired,' she said quickly, unwilling to spoil Dick's evening.

'But I am,' he smiled, and called for the bill.

Luckily there was no need to pass Benedict's table as they left the restaurant, and Sara breathed a sigh of relief when they reached the street. Yet though she could walk away from the man tonight, she wouldn't always be able to do so; if he *did* write for her, they'd inevitably be thrown together. But no matter how closely she had to work with him, she'd never allow him to shatter her life as he had her friend's.

She was her own woman, and that was how she intended to keep it.

CHAPTER FOUR

IN THE next six weeks Sara's life underwent a total transformation. In addition to her nightclub tour, she exchanged her tiny room in Battersea for an elegant three-bedroom apartment in Knightsbridge.

Not until she went to see it did she realise it was the show home, and exquisitely furnished by a top interior designer. But assuring her that she would be more than able to afford it with the proceeds of her first album, Dick advanced her the money to buy it.

Had she not been anxious about her mother, Sara would never have accepted his generosity, for she still harboured doubts about the lasting quality of her new career. But one look at her mother's face when she walked into Sara's apartment a week or so later made her glad she had done so.

Hardly had she seen her mother settled than she started her provincial tour.

The first time she stood in a dark, smoke-filled club before an audience more interested in food and drink than listening to someone sing, she wondered what the hell she had let herself in for. What chance did she have of capturing the attention of this gluttonous, hard-drinking crowd? She had no props to help her capture their attention; only herself and her voice.

Disregarding the microphone—she had no need of it in a room a fraction the size of the auditoriums she was used to—she stepped forward and began to sing, her clear tones overriding the clatter of knives and forks, the chatter of conversation.

At first only a few people paid attention to her, but soon there was total, appreciative silence that ended in sustained applause.

From then on Sara was never scared of an audience; not even the tough ones that proliferated throughout the Midlands. As Dick had said, it was a hard initiation—one where you either conquered or sank without trace—and there was no doubt, she conquered.

On the last night of her tour, he drove up to Birmingham to see her.

'You've done far better than I expected,' he said.

'And a hundred per cent better than *I* expected,' she confessed. 'I've learned how to judge an audience's mood, and I act accordingly.'

'Women are born actresses,' was his comment as he wandered round her dressing room while she removed her heavy make-up, preparatory to leaving.

'Is this the time of month you pay your alimony?' Sara teased, and he laughed and shook his head.

'I gave my ex a lump sum so I could forget about her.' He came a step closer to Sara. 'If you were fifteen years older, I might have offered you a different kind of contract.'

'I might have accepted it,' she said softly. 'You're a marshmallow man under your hard toffee exterior!'

Dick responded by putting a casual arm about her shoulders, and Sara hoped that despite his assertion to the contrary, he was not looking for more than a business relationship. But he released her after giving her a friendly hug, and urged her to get ready. They were only an hour's drive from London, and she had decided she would prefer to return home in the early hours of the morning rather than spend another night in a Midlands hotel.

'This was the toughest tour I've done,' she sighed as Dick's Rolls ate up the miles.

'There aren't any others on the agenda,' he assured her. 'From now on we'll concentrate on records and a few prestigious live appearances. Which reminds me, I'd like to take you to the first night of Benedict's show. I've got a box.'

'Colin's already sent me some tickets,' she told him, 'and I'm taking my mother.'

'You can both be my guests. You're more likely to be photographed if you're one of my party, and we need all the publicity we can get.'

'In that case I'll do as you say!'

'You're an independent young lady, aren't you?' he remarked. 'But I promise I'll only give you orders where your career's concerned. In all other respects, you're your own boss.'

Sara burst out laughing. Since her work looked like occupying her twenty-four hours out of twenty-four, he wasn't leaving her much time to 'do her own thing'.

It was after two o'clock when she let herself into her apartment. Though careful to make no noise, she had barely closed her bedroom door when a small figure in a fluffy dressing gown opened it again and came in with a cup of hot bouillon and a plate of smoked salmon sandwiches.

'Don't tell me you were waiting up for me!' Sara exclaimed, hugging her mother.

'Why shouldn't I? I moved in with you to look after you.'

Sara grinned, and wolfed down the sandwiches, only now realising how ravenous she was. She never ate before a show, and though Dick had offered to take her for a late supper, she had been too tired.

Kicking off her shoes, she collapsed on the bed and luxuriated in the beauty of the rose-pink walls and soft lighting that illuminated the finely polished woodwork and satin hangings; a far cry from the sparseness of her previous 'home'.

'Were you lonely here without me?' she asked, her eyes resting on the woman who was an older edition of herself.

'The first two weeks I could have cut my throat,' came Helen James' forthright reply. 'But since then I've made a few friends in the block, and I'm learning bridge, would you believe!'

'Good for you. It's time you started enjoying yourself. You can't mourn Dad for ever.'

Her mother's sigh spoke volumes, and Sara wondered whether she herself would feel the same all-encompassing love for a man as her mother had done. Right now, her career was the important thing.

'It was kind of Mr Cawthorne to drive up and collect you,' her mother said into the silence.

'He's protecting his investment!' grinned Sara.

'As long as he doesn't have any other motive. The pop scene's a pretty sordid one.'

'So are stockbroking and banking these days!' Sara teased, setting down her empty plate and yawning. 'I'm so exhausted I could stay in bed a week! You've no idea how tiring it is to project yourself to five hundred strange faces every night.'

'You can always give it up if it gets too much for you.'

'I can't just break my contract.' Sara stood up and slipped out of her dress.

'I suppose Mr Cawthorne's tied you hand and foot?'

'Dick's no tougher than any other record producer,' Sara said from the bathroom. 'Don't make him out an ogre, Mother. He's a darling man and you'll like him.'

'I doubt it. I can't bear pop music and I don't go for long hair and jeans.'

'That's not his style at all,' giggled Sara, wandering to

the door, toothbrush in hand. 'He's in his fifties!

'Even worse,' Helen James snorted. 'Blow-dried hair to hide the bald spot, and shirt open to his shrivelled navel.'

'That's Dick exactly,' Sara said without the vestige of a smile. 'You sure you haven't seen a picture of him?'

'I don't need to. Men in his profession are all the same.'

Sara thought of this conversation on Wednesday evening as she dressed for the première of the musical, and couldn't wait to see her mother's face when she actually met Dick! He'd be in for a surprise too, for she knew he was expecting to see a middle-aged *hausfrau*, not someone who could pass as Sara's older sister!

She was still dressing when Dick buzzed the intercom, and she pressed the button to let him in.

'I'm not ready yet,' she apologised, 'but I'll leave the front door ajar, so come in and fix yourself a drink.'

'Don't be too long,' he warned. 'There'll be a hell of a crush round the theatre.'

'Five minutes,' she promised, and was as good as her word, hurrying into the living room on a cloud of apricot chiffon and Arpège, to find him and her mother in animated conversation.

'I'll pay you back for the joke you played on me,' Helen James chided, and Dick's grin told Sara he knew how she'd described him.

'If you'd let me in on the joke,' he said, 'I'd have come in a wig and tartan dinner jacket!'

'And found yourself going to the theatre alone!' Sara quipped.

'Instead of with two beautiful women,' he added, his swift glance at Helen James bringing a blush to her cheeks.

Well, well, thought Sara, maybe a little matchmaking won't come amiss. I must see what I can do.

Sara had never been to a first night, nor had she anticipated that when she did, it would be to a Benedict Peters musical, where tickets were as hard to come by as gold nuggets. The pavements were awash with crowds anxious to see, the foyer with celebrities anxious to *be* seen.

To her surprise she came in for an immense amount of attention, and was interviewed for television by a gushing young man who commented about her boyfriend being in the show.

'Did *you* tell him that?' Sara reproached Dick as they mounted the thickly carpeted stairs to their box.

'Blame it on our publicity department,' he shrugged.

'Well, please inform them I'm trying to get Colin *out* of my life—not more involved in it!'

'Yes, boss!' Placatingly Dick put his hand on her arm, and kept it there until he ushered her into her seat.

Peering down at the audience filing in, Sara immediately saw Benedict with a well-known and beautiful socialite. Her hackles rose at the sight of his dark, saturnine features.

Was he experiencing any first-night nerves, she wondered, or was he so used to success that he took it for granted? Much as she disliked him, she could not blame him for feeling confident, for everything he touched brought him acclaim.

'That tall man talking to Albert Finney,' her mother murmured. 'Wasn't he one of the judges on your talent show?'

'Yes.' Sara tried to sound non-committal. 'It's Benedict Peters.'

'He's extremely good-looking.' Mrs James' attention was still focused on the composer and, as if on cue, he looked directly up at the box.

Sara saw his startled expression, and with amusement

realised that from this distance he must have thought he
was seeing double!

'Sara, my dear.'

Dick touched her shoulder and she turned round to be
introduced to his other two guests, the lead singers from
Sage and Onions, the group Benedict admired so much.

Only when they were all seated did she hear Dick
whisper to her mother that Gerry and Inge had been
married ten years, and as Sara flung him a questioning
look, he smiled.

'I was just proving to your mother that not all pop stars
change partners every time they change their clothes!'

Sara laughed, stifling it as the orchestra struck up the
overture, and they all settled back to enjoy the show.

How banal was the word 'enjoy' to describe three hours
of pure pleasure! Even Sara, who thought she knew the
score well, marvelled at how different it now sounded.
Since she had left the chorus, new songs had been added,
several taken out, and some considerably altered.

Though she didn't like Carol Dean as a person, she had to
admit she made an excellent Magda—a swinging 1980s
girl who falls for a missionary and convinces him she has
genuinely 'seen the light'.

Colin and Ella Brown played her brother and his
girlfriend, small-time crooks involved in what they
believed to be the biggest swindle of their lives, and anxious
to enlist Magda's help in their scheme. After many amusing
twists, all ended well, with the young couple winning a
fortune and turning over a pious new leaf, and Magda
sailing off to a happy future, Bible in hand.

Carol played the role for laughs, though Sara would have
wrung more pathos from the part. But the audience didn't
share her opinion, and there was thunderous applause at

the end, and a tumultuous reception for Benedict, when he came on stage.

'He's invited us to his first-night party at the Savoy,' Dick announced as the curtain finally came down, and though it was the last thing Sara wanted, there was no way she could refuse to go.

Entering the glittering River Room Suite and seeing the adoring crowds jostling around the composer, she was hard put not to throw her glass of champagne in his face.

Her mother, ever receptive to her mood, gave her a warning frown, and Sara forced a smile to her lips as she went forward to congratulate him.

'I'm so glad you came,' he murmured, the sardonic gleam in his eyes showing he knew what an effort it cost her to be polite to him.

Before Sara could say anything, a luscious blonde flung herself at him, and he neatly evaded the provocative red mouth while managing to greet her with equal warmth. Seeing the girl clinging to his arm, Sara thought angrily that this should have been Barbie's place—except that her friend would have hated the glitzy glamour and phoney effervescence of this first-night crowd. Was that why their relationship had foundered? Because Benedict had known she wouldn't fit in with his lifestyle?

Turning away from him, Sara came face to face with Colin. Only then could her pleasure in the show's success be heartfelt, for she knew it marked the beginning of his career which, from now on—short of a disaster—would be up, up and away.

'Wasn't it great!' he grinned, hugging her, his skin flushed with excitement.

'Do you need me to answer that?' she laughed, and he shook his head and pushed a way clear for them to a relatively quiet corner of the room, and a window overlooking the dark, gleaming river.

'I can't wait to see the morning's reviews,' he said. 'Care to come to Fleet Street for the early editions?'

'Do you need confirmation of the obvious? This show will run for years.'

'Security at last,' he said dramatically. 'Marry me, Sara, and make this my luckiest night.'

'It is,' she said lightly. 'I'm turning you down!'

His reply was forestalled by Ella coming over to greet Sara, and Colin moved off in search of champagne for them.

'Colin's as thrilled by your success as his own,' Ella remarked, watching his departing back. 'But then you're very special to him.'

'Only because we've known each other since our student days,' Sara shrugged. 'It forms a kind of bond.'

'It's more than that. He's in love with you.'

'It's become a habit with him. And habits should be changed. So feel free to have a go!'

'I'd lose out.' A wry smile crossed Ella's pixie face, and she ran her fingers through her curly black hair, touselling it more than ever. 'He can't see me for the stars in his eyes when he looks at *you*.'

'Don't you know the proverb about faint heart never winning ...'

'Which I heartily endorse,' a deep voice said behind them, and Sara had no need to turn to know who it was.

'I can't imagine *you* being faint-hearted,' she remarked as Benedict Peters came into her line of vision.

'Wait till you know me better.'

She longed to say this was the last thing she wanted, and had Ella not been there, would have taken great delight in telling him Barbie was her best friend.

'Let's cut the personal talk and be professional,' he said

smoothly. 'I'm interested in your opinion of tonight's performance.'

'It was excellent—as I'm sure the reviews will endorse.'

'I'd still like an insider's comment,' he persisted. 'I rarely take notice of theatre critics. Give me your honest opinion, Sara.'

Convinced he was baiting her, Sara was all set to do so and damn the consequences, when she glimpsed Dick talking to her mother, and knew he'd be furious with her if she didn't guard her tongue.

'Every performer puts their own stamp on what they do,' she hedged, 'and ten actors will give you ten different performances. The main thing is that the show jelled as a whole. A change in nuance here and there means nothing.'

'I don't agree,' Benedict said incisively, surprising her by the seriousness with which he took her comment. 'A wrong nuance can throw the entire concept out of gear. Like a loose bolt in a machine. So tell me which bolts *you* noticed?'

'None,' Sara lied.

'I don't believe you.'

'Why not?'

'Because your eyes are flickering—and that's a dead giveaway! But as you're scared of speaking your mind— which I must say surprises me—I'll leave you.'

He moved away, and Sara breathed a sigh of relief, still puzzled as to why he had wanted her opinion. Not for an instant had she believed he really valued it.

'He's such a nice person,' Ella said sincerely. 'Although he knows his word is law when it comes to the show, he never throws his weight around.'

'If his word is law, he doesn't have to!'

Sara wasn't aware of how sharp she had sounded until she saw Ella's startled expression, and was glad Colin chose that moment to return, champagne bottle in hand.

'Sorry to be so long,' he mumbled, slightly the worse for wear. 'But I was waylaid by a reporter.'

'With bright orange lipstick,' retorted Ella, rubbing his cheek with a tissue.

Grinning, he refilled their glasses, and Sara chattered gaily, saying all the right things, yet wondering how soon she could leave.

In the end her mother provided her with the excuse, coming over to murmur that she had a splitting headache and was going home.

'I'll come with you,' Sara said and, overriding her mother's objection that she didn't need a nursemaid, went in search of Dick.

'I was ready to leave an hour ago,' he confessed, 'but you seemed to be enjoying yourself so much I didn't want to tear you away from your friends.'

'We should work out better signals,' grinned Sara as they descended the stairs to the lobby.

'Wait here while I get a taxi,' Dick said. 'I sent my chauffeur home.'

'How about a stroll along the Embankment first?' she suggested. 'It might blow away Mother's headache.'

'Some fresh air sounds wonderful,' Helen James agreed. 'Crowds and stuffy atmospheres aren't my scene.'

'Nor mine,' Dick responded.

'Is that possible in your line of business?'

He raised a rueful eyebrow. 'You seem determined to see me in a particular light, Mrs James.'

'My fault again,' Sara interposed. 'I gave Mother the impression you were a racy character!'

He shook his head goodhumouredly. 'When two women gang up on me, what can I do but give in!'

They walked along the Embankment till they reached Waterloo Bridge, where Dick hailed a cab. Within moments they drew up outside the Knightsbridge apartment block, and he kissed Sara on the cheek, then turned to her mother, raising her hand to his lips.

'It was a pleasure meeting you, Mrs James. I hope we can repeat this evening.'

'I'm sure we'll be seeing each other now you're looking after Sara's career,' Helen James said coolly, and hurried into the lobby.

'Dick was only being friendly,' protested Sara, following her mother. 'I thought you rather rebuffed him.'

'I didn't mean to. But it's a long while since anyone kissed my hand, and it rather floored me.'

Mulling this over as she prepared for bed, Sara reflected that all things considered, her mother and Dick had got on rather well. As indeed she wanted them to. Dick was charming and divorced, her mother charming and widowed, and who knew where this could lead?

CHAPTER FIVE

SARA met Dick the following afternoon in his opulent office in Holland Park, atop the modern glass and steel skyscraper that housed his record company.

Tony was there when she arrived, almost lost in a vast leather settee—one of many that dotted the large area in front of Dick's desk—and he rose and came towards her.

'Dick and I were discussing the two numbers for your single, and we both think they should be——'

'Benedict's,' Sara cut in.

'We've several numbers for you to choose from,' Dick pacified.

'I'll leave it to you,' she shrugged. 'You know the market better than I do.'

The two men went into a brief conference, after which Dick called in Larry Day, the dynamic thirty-year-old who headed the publicity department, to discuss how best to promote the record.

'With a video,' he said emphatically. 'With Sara's face and figure I'd like to put her on a beach in Tobago, surrounded by well-muscled men. And of course if she sings "Swimming Against the Tide", we can have her rising from the sea like Aphrodite.'

And as scantily dressed, Sara thought mutinously, deciding this was one suggestion she wouldn't go along with. But before she could say so, Dick forestalled her.

'No, Larry. Having a girl drop her clothes is the obvious way to get attention, and you're too highly paid for me to let you get away with the easy option!'

'Point taken,' grinned Larry. 'Give me a day and I'll come up with something else!'

The video he eventually devised had Sara gliding on ice in the arms of a world championship skater—with an understudy doing the skating—and hang-gliding over the Alps in a white silk Zandra Rhodes creation—by courtesy of the same understudy.

It was the most hectic time she had spent, and she practically staggered into the studio to start rehearsing with Tony the day after her return from the Swiss Alps.

Tony was as ruthless as when he had coached her for the talent show, but after four long days he pronounced himself satisfied, and recording began.

The first side went without a hitch. Three takes and it was done. But the second had a section where she was accompanied by a lone flute, and no matter how hard she tried to reach the end of the phrase simultaneously with the instrument, she couldn't manage it.

'Well try it once more from the top,' Tony said, 'and if we don't get it, we'll record you and the flute separately, then do a mix.'

Knowing there was an alternative did wonders for Sara's nerves, and five minutes later the second side was successfully completed and they went into the recording engineer's glass-fronted studio to listen to it.

Sara knew nothing about the intricacies of cutting a modern-day record, beyond the fact that electronic wizardry enabled one sound engineer to do the work of six, while tape decks, splicing machines, amplifiers, and eight- and ten-track recorders could change a voice out of all recognition, even to making it seem as if it were backed by its own chorus!

Sara's work was now over, though not Tony's, for he would be spending long hours with the recordist, splicing one take on to another, highlighting one instrument, softening a second, until the final disc—which often bore little resemblance to the original—was completed.

'I'd no idea it was so complicated,' she confessed. 'It

makes a singer feel extraneous!'

'Some singers are,' the recordist grinned. 'I could name a few who'd never dare give a live performance! Present company excepted,' he added.

'I endorse, that.' Tony chucked her lightly under the chin. 'You're set for stardom, Sara—and fast!'

Bearing out Tony's prediction, her single was a sell-out within a week of its release. It was hard not to let her new-found fame go to her head, but she warned herself how transient success could be in this branch of the entertainment business.

Colin dismissed her pessimism completely, and insisted on taking her out to celebrate.

'Come see the show first—I'll leave a ticket for you at the box office—then we'll go on to Annabel's.'

Only as she arrived at the theatre did Sara realise the possibility of bumping into Benedict. But luckily there was no sign of him, and with a sigh of relief she slipped into her seat as the curtain rose.

Great though the first night had been, the show was even better now it had settled into its natural rhythm. Carol was still playing her part for laughs, which Sara still didn't like—but Colin's performance was far more developed.

He and Ella made a great team, but half-way through the second act the girl's voice seemed to weaken, while the colour on her cheeks stood out in bright patches. Colin hurriedly took up the refrain and Ella nestled silently in his arms, which Sara didn't remember her doing on the first night. It could be a new piece of business, but somehow she doubted it.

Her conviction was confirmed when she went backstage after the finale and saw Ella being carried out of the stage door on a stretcher.

'What's wrong with her, Colin?' she asked, hurrying into his dressing room.

'It's her gall bladder.' His movements were jerky as he

slapped cold cream on his face and removed his make-up with a tissue. 'It's been playing her up for months and she'll probably have to have it out.'

'It's not a serious operation these days,' Sara soothed.

'I know. But she had to pull out of her last show because of a broken ankle, and if she gets the reputation of being jinxed, she'll be finished.'

'Don't be silly!'

'I'm not. You know how superstitious everyone is in this business.'

Sara sought for a way to reassure him. 'How about giving Annabel's a miss and going to the hospital?' she suggested. 'Then you can hear exactly how she is.'

'Would you mind?' he said gratefully. 'I'll feel much easier once I've seen her settled. We needn't stay long.'

Some half hour later they were talking to the Night Sister on Women's Surgical, who told them Ella was to be operated on in the morning.

'If you'd care to have a word with her . . .' she concluded.

'You go without me,' Sara told Colin, deciding it would be good for Ella's morale to know he had been worried enough to rush over to see her. She only hoped he wouldn't mention that *she* was outside!

Alone in the corridor she paced restlessly up and down. Colin was more worried about Ella than the facts justified, and she suspected his feelings for the girl ran deeper than he realised.

Someone in a dark suit stepped out of the lift, and her heart thumped heavily as she recognised Benedict. Strange how, even from this distance, she knew him. Dislike must give her sensitive antennae!

Not so him, for he was almost upon her before he realised she was there.

'Sara! I didn't expect to see you.'

She didn't add that she was equally surprised to see *him*. This sort of crisis was usually dealt with by the producer, with someone in Benedict's position satisfying themselves by sending flowers.

'I came with Colin,' she told him.

'Oh, there you are, Mr Peters!'

Night Sister descended on him like a long-lost relation, and, listening to the conversation, Sara gathered he had been here earlier and had left to make arangements for Ella to be moved to the private wing. His solicitude surprised her yet again, for it seemed so out of character.

'I don't think your thoughts are very flattering to me,' he said wryly, as Night Sister left them.

Annoyed that he found her so readable, Sara flushed. 'I didn't expect you to come here personally. I thought you'd be too busy.'

'I'm busy with my business—which happens to be this musical and everything and everyone connected with it. Even *you*, if you were in a show of mine, would merit my attention!'

'I'm glad to hear it,' Sara sniffed. 'But it's hardly likely to arise.'

His mouth tightened and he turned away, then thinking better of it, he swung round on her. 'The way we're going on is ridiculous. If you're still angry with me because I once made a perfectly justifiable criticism of your voice, then——'

'It's more than that,' she cut in. 'I simply find you overbearing, autocratic and phoney.'

'Phoney?'

'Yes, Mr Peters—phoney!'

He looked so affronted, she was hard put not to laugh. Autocratic and overbearing he had accepted without the blink of an eyelid, but he balked at being called phoney!

'I know I can be overbearing and autocratic when it comes to my work, but that's because I know what I want and I won't settle for second best. But in my private life I try to be neither. As to my being a phoney—that's an accusation no one's levelled at me before. I——' He stopped as Colin came into the corridor.

'Hello, Benedict. Sister says you're having Ella moved to a private room. That's damned decent of you.'

'Not at all. The cast's insured, so she might as well have the best!'

Colin swivelled round as a nurse approached them, and Benedict gave Sara an ironic smile.

'You see you needn't put my behaviour down to kindness of heart—merely to my having a good insurance policy!'

'I'm glad to know my judgement of you isn't wrong!'

'Nor mine of you. You've got a golden voice, my angel, but the tongue of a viper!'

Sara trembled visibly with fury, but Colin was too engrossed with the nurse to notice, and she was in control of herself when he turned back to her.

'They've given Ella a painkiller and she's too drowsy to know what's going on, so we might as well push off to Annabel's.

'I can give you a lift if you like.' This from Benedict. 'I'm going there myself.'

'That's great,' smiled Colin, and Sara, hiding her abhorrence at having to accept his offer, silently went with the two men to the front entrance of the hospital where a silver-grey Ferrari was parked.

'I thought you had a Mercedes,' she said involuntarily, and saw Benedict give her a sharp look.

'It was involved in an accident and I sold it.'

'A bad accident?' she asked with pseudo-innocence.

'Bad enough. How come you knew what car I had?'

'I—er—I read about it. That's the price of fame, you know. Everything you have, say and do becomes public property.'

'It's the negative aspect of success,' he agreed, unlocking the car.

Sara quickly climbed into the back, surreptitiously motioning Colin to the front, and they set off.

Surprisingly, Benedict was a very careful driver, and though several cars, drawing alongside him at various traffic signals, seemed eager to give him a run for his money, he refused to rise to the challenge.

'That's the trouble driving a Ferrari,' he muttered. 'There's always some bloody fool ready to cut you up.'

'Then why have one?' Sara couldn't help asking.

'Because I go abroad a lot and use autobahns and motor routes. But I think I'll get a small runabout for town.'

They drew to a stop in Berkeley Square. Much as Sara had looked forward to visiting Annabel's, knowing Benedict was going to be here had taken away the pleasure, and she would gladly have cried off. Yet if she did, it would ruin Colin's evening, to say nothing of giving Benedict a good laugh, for he was astute enough to see through any excuse she gave for not going in.

The instant they stepped into the entrance he was swallowed up by a crowd of well-heeled, well-dressed aristocrats—if their high-pitched voices and braying laughter was anything to go by.

It confirmed her suspicion that this was the milieu he came from, and the knowledge that he had never had to starve in a garret before achieving success, intensified her dislike of him. Damn! If she didn't watch out she'd become paranoid about him. After all, he wasn't the only man who'd behaved badly towards a woman—it was a run-of-the-mill story these days, and she shouldn't let it needle her.

Once inside the disco, she made certain she and Colin sat as far away from him as possible, though whenever they went on to the floor she could not avoid seeing him, each time with a different girl.

Well, why not? He was world-famous, rich as Croesus and handsome as Adonis. The last attribute alone would have got him all the women he wanted, yet he had all three!

No wonder he was footloose and never—as Dick had told her—made the mistake of marrying the vapid women who chased him.

'You're so beautiful,' Colin said thickly, breaking into her thoughts. 'Why won't you——'

The wild beat of a bongo drowned him out, and Sara grimaced and left the floor. Though uninhibited on stage, in her personal life she was shy, and would no more have indulged in the extreme gyrations going on around her than she would have rocketed to the moon.

Not so Benedict. To her amazement he flung himself energetically into the rhythm, strong legs twisting and turning, hands firm on the supple body of his partner. It was a blatantly sexual dance, its eroticism increased by the clapping of an admiring audience who had stepped back to watch the performance.

'The girl's Marly Roberts,' Colin informed Sara, naming the younger daughter of a Cabinet Minister. 'She's Benedict's latest.'

He certainly went for variety, Sara thought. Carol, with hair like midnight, this one flaxen as a cotton field—and ready for the picking.

'Let's get out of here,' she said abruptly. 'The noise is giving me a headache.'

It was a relief to finally return home, having adroitly escaped amorous overtures from Colin by backing into the lift as he leaned forward to catch hold of her. How she hoped he would turn to Ella once the girl had recovered and was back on stage.

Tonight had shown her more clearly than ever that they had no future together, and she wondered if she would ever meet a man with whom she would care to share her life.

Maybe her career was more important to her than she had realised. But even as she thought this, she knew it wasn't true. Far more likely that her parents' idyllic marriage had made it impossible for her to settle for anything less than perfect.

But surely somewhere in the world was a man she could love with all her heart, and who would love her in the same way? Her success would be meaningless if she had to enjoy it alone.

On this sobering admission, she turned out the light and went to sleep.

CHAPTER SIX

ELLA BROWN's illness brought Benedict back into the limelight, and he was photographed with Linda, the understudy who had taken over the part.

And taken it over very well, if press notices were anything to go by, though Colin was less than enthused.

'She's over-acting and under-singing,' he complained when he had dinner at Sara's apartment the following Sunday. 'And I swear she lives on a diet of garlic. When I kiss her in the last act, I have to hold my breath! I wish *you'd* taken over the part,' he added. 'At least then I'd get to kiss you!'

'I'm an onion girl myself!' said Sara, straight-faced, 'and you'd hate it!'

'Try me.'

'No, Colin. We're friends, nothing more. If you can't accept that . . .'

'I do.' His sigh came from the heart. 'You're a bright star that will never shine for me; that I'll have to watch glittering from afar.'

'Oh, Colin, I'm so sorry,' she sighed.

'So am I. At one time I thought we'd end up together, but now . . . Well, I don't know any longer what you're looking for.'

Neither do I, Sara thought disconsolately when he had gone. What was it Colin had likened her to? A bright star glittering from afar. She frowned unhappily. This was how she was beginning to think of herself; as a star glittering for everyone, yet for no one in particular. She had admirers in plenty, but no one to whom she felt special, or who she

57

wanted to feel special towards *her.*

What's the matter with me? she chided herself. I've fame, money and a wonderful career. I should be counting my blessings, not mourning my miseries.

She was still sitting in the lounge, lost in thought, when her mother returned from a bridge lesson.

'Why did Colin leave so early?' she wanted to know.

'He finally accepted that we've no future together,' Sara told her.

'Pity. He's a sweet man.'

'Sweet men can be awfully tedious. It's older ones with a past who are exciting!'

'Thinking of anyone special?' her mother asked.

'Not really.' Sara stacked the dishes on the trolley and wheeled it into the kitchen. 'Which reminds me,' she called out, 'Dick's invited us to spend next weekend on his yacht.'

'I like your train of thought,' her mother said from the doorway, and it took a few seconds for Sara to catch her meaning.

'You're right,' she chuckled. 'Dick's very attractive and he does have a past . . .'

'Indeed?'

'Not too lurid, though! Just one wife, whom he divorced ten years ago. It's a pity he's never remarried. He has everything to offer.'

Her mother shrugged uninterestedly. 'I'm not sure I fancy a weekend away. Anyway, he's only invited me because of you.'

'He didn't need to, you know. We're not Siamese twins! Now no more arguing. You'll thoroughly enjoy yourself once we're there.' Seeing her mother's still mutinous expression, Sara added: 'If you won't go, then neither will I.'

'Don't be silly!' Helen protested.

'It's silly for you to turn down the invitation.'

'You're blackmailing me, Sara.'

'I know.'

'Very well, I'll go,' sighed her mother.

It was such a grudging acceptance, Sara knew there was no way she could persuade her mother to buy cruise wear for the trip. But that didn't mean she wouldn't have any, for as Sara shopped for herself later that week, she bought for two!

Friday noon found them in Folkestone, aboard *Solo*, Dick's hundred-and-fifty-foot yacht, having flown there from London's heliport. It was like stepping into another world, and Sara gasped at her first glimpse of its luxury. Never in her wildest dreams had she anticipated such opulence.

There were three decks: one for crew, the second for guest suites and the top one for reception rooms. Here was the dining room with its magnificent malachite table that rivalled the one Sara had seen in the Vatican during a weekend holiday trip to Rome; a sumptuous main salon furnished in beige and brown biscuit colours, and Dick's sycamore-panelled stateroom, which she glimpsed through the half-open door, with its navy blue tailored coverlet on the wide bed, and matching blue and white curtains at windows that overlooked a private sun-deck.

The five guest suites were furnished in pastels, with colour coming from the Chinese lamps and ornaments in the wall niches at either side of the beds.

After Sara had unpacked, she went across the gangway to see her mother. The stateroom was empty and she put the cruise wear she had bought her on the bed—slacks and tops, sundress, and a peach silk dinner dress.

She was on the point of leaving when her mother emerged from the bathroom, wrapped in soft terry towelling.

'I thought only oil sheiks lived like this! My bath is large enough to swim in!'

'I've got two tubs,' Sara grinned. 'A his and a hers!'

Chuckling, her mother ambled to the bed, her smile fading as she saw the clothes on it. 'What's all this?'

'A present for you, darling.'

'Well, you can take them straight back! I'm not a charity case and I won't be treated as one. I can afford to buy my own clothes!'

'For heaven's sake, Mother! All I did was get you a few outfits. That's half the fun of having money—so you can spend it on people you love.'

'I'd rather you spent it on yourself—or better still, save it. The public's fickle, Sara, and what's popular today could be a flop tomorrow.'

'Still doubtful of your daughter's success, Helen?'

The two women spun round to see Dick in the doorway. In navy shorts and a pale blue top that made his sandy hair look redder, he was surprisingly well muscled and firm of flesh, his sinewy legs thrust into open thonged sandals.

'I couldn't help overhearing,' he apologised, his eyes moving from one woman to the other, before coming to rest on the bed.

The look on his face told Sara he had overheard more than a few words, and she said quickly, 'Mother's annoyed because I bought her a few things.'

'So I gathered. But most people enjoy being independent. You should remember that, Sara.'

'She was simply being generous,' her mother intervened, instantly defensive. 'Even as a child she used to give her toys away.' She glanced at her daughter, then tentatively touched the dresses on the bed. 'They're lovely, darling, and—and I'm sorry I was so ungracious about accepting them.'

'That's all right, Mother—I understand.'

'Can I take it my two favourite women are no longer

quarrelling?' asked Dick with a slight smile.

'My daughter and I don't quarrel,' came the stiff reply as Helen James bundled up the clothes and marched over to the wardrobe.

Raising an eyebrow at Sara, Dick went on his way, calling over his shoulder, 'I'll see you both on the sun-deck.'

Sara watched her mother in silence for a moment, then blurted out: 'Dick wasn't interfering, you know. He was merely trying to smooth things over.'

'I realise that. But I always overreact to him. I'll try to be more careful in future. Now give me a few minutes to change and I'll join you.'

As Sara went out, Helen James bit back a sigh. She had promised to watch her step with Dick, but she was by no means sure she could.

Although she appreciated why her daughter enjoyed going out with him, she was deeply disturbed that Sara saw him to the exclusion of anyone else. For Dick it was undoubtedly an ego trip to squire such a beautiful young girl, but he was far too old for her, and should know better than to take up all her spare time.

Pushing her thoughts aside, she donned the slacks Sara had bought her. They were more figure-fitting than she would have chosen for herself, though she had to admit they suited her; as did the cherry-coloured top, which gave warmth to her skin. She didn't know why she'd been so angry with Sara for buying the clothes, except that for the last few months she had felt edgy among all these show business people.

'Oh, Alan,' she said aloud. 'If only you hadn't died so young!' Determinedly suppressing her morbid thoughts, she picked up her straw handbag and went out.

Reaching the sun-deck, part of it shaded by a beige and white striped awning that matched the covers on the white wicker lounging chairs, she saw that a table had been set up for lunch and a white-coated steward was giving a final polish to the sparkling wine glasses.

Helen heard voices, a man's she did not recognise, and was astonished to see Benedict Peters coming towards her.

Having only seen him twice—from a distance at the première of his show, and at the party afterwards—she was stunned at how good-looking he was close up. His casual denims emphasised his broad-shouldered, slim-hipped body, and he exuded a virility that left her breathless. If he did that to a woman of forty-seven, who should know better, Lord only knew what he did to a twenty-year-old!

'I'm not going to say the obvious,' he smiled.

'I'm glad to hear it. Not every middle-aged lady likes to be taken for her daughter!' she smiled back.

He laughed. 'Wasn't it Shaw who said youth is too good to waste on the young?'

'What's all this talk about age?' interposed Dick, coming from under the awning to join them.

His glance approved Helen's outfit, and she stiffened, resenting the unexpected intimacy of his gaze, and glad to see Sara come through the main saloon, her flushed cheeks giving away her annoyance at finding Benedict here. She could understand it, though, for a few days ago Sara had told her of his involvement with Barbie, and how badly he had behaved.

Ignoring the man completely, Sara concentrated on Dick, leaning towards him with an air of intimacy as he placed a glass of champagne in her hand.

Abruptly Helen moved away from them to lean over the rail, hearing them speaking together softly, though she could not make out what they were saying. Someone came to stand beside her, and she saw it was Benedict.

'You must be very proud of your daughter, Mrs James.'

'Helen,' she said. 'And I am—very. I always felt she'd

make it, though not in this field. She trained as an opera singer, you know.'

'I didn't. But now you've told me, it explains a lot of things. I suppose you know she was in the chorus of my show, and why she left it?'

'Yes, indeed!'

'I'm afraid she's no fan of mine.'

Helen longed to tell him exactly why, but instead said, 'With all your millions of fans, I'm sure you won't miss one.'

His shrug brought into play the muscles across his wide chest. He really was a devastating creature, she thought. If only I were fifteen years younger, or he fifteen years older ...

'Lunch is ready!' their host called, and Helen, swinging round, caught the warm glance Sara was giving Dick.

She was glad when the meal—delicious though it was— was over and she could retire to a lounger and make a pretence of sunbathing.

'Better be careful,' Dick warned, coming to stand beside her, 'The rays are much stronger when they're reflected off the sea.'

'I'm wearing a barrier cream, thanks.' She avoided his eyes and focusing on a point beyond him, realised the yacht was moving.

'Where are we going?' she asked.

'To have dinner at Le Touquet.' He drew a stool close and straddled it.

'It's years since I've been to France,' she said quickly, anxious to avoid an intimate tête-à-tête. 'Alan—my husband—was a keen fisherman, and we always took our holidays in Scotland.'

'You like fishing?'

'Not especially. But Alan was so fond of it I didn't have the heart to tell him.'

'So you suffered in silence?'

'Hardly suffered. If my husband was happy, so was I.'

Dick smiled. 'I'm sure today's woman would berate you for not doing your own thing!'

'I wonder. They talk emancipation, and probably act on it in their careers, but when it comes to the man they love——'

'They put a ring through his nose and lead him where they will!' Benedict's deep voice finished for her, and she looked round, laughing.

'That's a very cynical comment,' Dick protested.

'I'm a cynical man.'

'You'll eat your words when you fall in love.'

'I fall in love every week!' Benedict shrugged.

'You mean you have sex every week,' Dick said bluntly.

Benedict grinned and peeled off his shirt to reveal bronze skin, shiny as satin, with a thick mat of hair disappearing in a V beneath the belt of his slacks.

'Affairs suit me fine,' he said. 'A light-hearted relationship with no recriminations when it's over. Unlike love, which ties you hand and foot—usually to a money-spending machine!'

Seeing Sara's indignant expression—she was sitting a few yards away—Helen was scared her daughter would cast discretion to the winds, which could make for an embarrassing scene, and said hurriedly,

'I think Dick's right. You're only a cynic because you don't know what love is. And I'm willing to bet that when you do, you'll fall twice as hard as anyone else.'

'I doubt that very much. But I get the impression everyone here is waiting to see me come a cropper!'

'They certainly are,' chuckled Dick. 'And I agree with Helen. Like the reformed rake who becomes a priest, I see you pushing a pram in St James' Park!'

Benedict gave a throaty laugh and lay back to sun himself. Helen followed suit, and after a moment, heard

Dick move away. Only then did she relax and enjoy the soft breeze that rippled over her face as the yacht breasted the Channel waters. The sea was calm as glass, and above her, seagulls emitted their cries.

She was smiling at the thought of Benedict falling in love when she heard Sara's laugh, followed by Dick's measured tone, and her pleasure faded. Determinedly she concentrated on the moment: the sea breeze, the smell of warm wood, the soft slither of the steward's feet as he moved around.

At four-thirty tea was served, and remembering she had promised Sara she'd be friendlier to Dick, Helen forced herself to smile at him as he came over to join her.

'It's a good thing I'm only here for the weekend,' she said, helping herself to some bite-sized coffee éclairs, 'or yours would be the only yacht with a barge on board!'

'Stay a week and you can choose your own menus!'

'Sara couldn't get away that long—you work her too hard.'

'You can always come on your own.'

Sara chose that moment to join them, fresh as a daisy in a lemon and white sundress.

'What are you two gossiping about?' she enquired.

'Aren't we allowed our secrets?' chided Dick, and for answer got his hair ruffled.

Disturbed by the intimacy, Helen murmured that she'd had too much sun and went down to her stateroom. But even there she could not rid herself of the stifling feeling that had surged up in her at seeing the rapport between her daughter and Dick.

It was still in her mind when Sara walked in, her slenderness covered by a silky green kimono.

'Feeling better, Mum?'

'Much,' Helen lied.

'Good. We'll be going ashore at seven-thirty. Dick's booked a table at Le Poisson d'Or. It's one of the best fish restaurants in Le Touquet, so wear your new dress.'

'I wouldn't dare wear anything else!'

At a quarter past seven, nervous yet composed, Helen went on deck. They had already docked in the harbour, which seemed chock-a-block with hundreds of craft, some small, some large, yet none as striking as *Solo*. Helen felt self-conscious, aware that her clinging coloured dress gave her a look of sensuality she felt unbecoming to a woman of what the French called 'a certain age'.

'You look stunning,' said Dick, coming up behind her.

Helen whirled round to see him regarding her with unfeigned pleasure. Colour bloomed in her face and he gave a soft laugh.

'Blushing's a rare quality in a woman these days.'

'In the young perhaps. Not for my generation.'

'*Our* generation,' he corrected.

She was at a loss to know how to reply, and was relieved to see Sara and Benedict approach.

It was clear the two of them had had some altercation, for her daughter's red chiffon matched the flags of temper in her cheeks, while Benedict's suave manner failed to disguise the tautness about his mouth.

Dick noticed it too, for he suggested they have an aperitif in the restaurant, rather than on board, and marshalled them quickly down the gangplank to a waiting limousine.

Within minutes they reached a restaurant whose terrace was built directly over the beach, the glow from its windows spilling out on the sand.

Dick was obviously well known here, for the *patron* greeted him with a broad smile and ushered them to a corner table on the terrace, where a magnum of champagne was cooling in an ice bucket.

In the warm, elegant atmosphere of impeccable white linen, silver cutlery and glittering glassware, they all visibly relaxed, and Helen's fears that the evening would turn out a disaster disappeared.

Their dinner was superb: lightly poached scallops in a tarragon sauce, followed by grilled lobster, and concluded by an assortment of fruit sorbets served with crisp almond *tuiles*. Conversation ebbed and flowed, no one touching on anything serious lest it spoil the mood, and it was only when coffee and brandy were served that Dick turned the conversation to the theatre.

'Your musical looks set to break all records, Benedict,' he commented as he lit up a cheroot. 'Correct me if I'm wrong, but I don't recall you ever having a flop.'

'I haven't.' It was an unequivocal reply.

'Shouldn't you touch wood when you say that?' Sara asked, looking at him with ill-concealed antipathy.

'Why? I'm not superstitious. One makes one's own luck.'

'You can't mean that! I know loads of talented singers and musicians who've slogged for years without getting anywhere. And they've tried everything to get to the top!'

'They may *think* they have. But more often than not it's a question of seeing an oppportunity and grasping it; of being willing to go out on a limb. The way you did, for example.'

Sara shrugged, her amber-gold hair swinging round her shoulders as she leaned forward. 'I had two fairy godmothers—or should I say godfathers?—waving their wands for me. Tony and Dick.'

'How about being Sara's third godfather,' Dick threw the younger man a humorous glance, 'and writing some numbers for the album she'll be doing?'

There was a momentary silence, then Benedict reached for his wine glass. 'I stopped writing pop stuff years ago,' he shrugged.

'I was thinking of ballads. Possibly even something with a message.'

'Spare me that! I'm just a simple composer.'

'What modesty!' mocked Sara.

'It's my most likeable characteristic,' Benedict agreed, his mouth quirking. 'If I'd been born in the reign of Elizabeth the First rather than the Second, I'd have been a wandering minstrel.'

'On a superb Arab stallion that you stabled in a castle in Spain!' Sara replied so promptly that he burst out laughing.

'You persist in having your own distorted picture of me, don't you? But I assure you a mandolin and an old nag would suit me fine—and no tax inspector to harass me either!'

'I'll harass you instead,' Dick interposed. 'No one interprets your work better than Sara—you've said so yourself—and it would be a shame if you two didn't collaborate.'

'Benedict doesn't need me,' Sara said quietly, touching Dick's hand and then leaving it there. 'And with you looking after my career, I'm sure I don't need *him!*'

'Spoken like a realist!' Benedict raised his glass to her, and Dick shrugged and signalled for the bill.

The streets were quiet as they walked back to the harbour. Sara paired with Dick, while Benedict joined Helen, and seemed to deliberately slow his step to put them several yards behind.

'Are you?' he asked Helen.

'What?' With a start she realised she hadn't heard a word he had said. 'I'm sorry, I was miles away.'

'This clearly isn't my evening!'

'Oh, please! I didn't mean to be rude. But I—I was thinking of Sara and her career.'

'Which is what I was talking about! I asked if you were annoyed with me for turning down Dick's offer?'

'Disappointed, rather than annoyed. After all, it's your prerogative.'

'You think I don't want to help her?'

'Do you?' countered Helen, throwing caution to the wind. 'After all, why make such a fuss about a couple of songs? From what I've read about you, you can—er— what's the word—"knock one off" in as long as it takes you to set it down on paper!'

'You shouldn't believe everything you read,' came the whimsical reply. 'Sometimes it doesn't even take me that long!'

'Then why——?'

'Because sometimes it takes a damn sight longer! Particularly lately, when I've become bored by the stuff.' Benedict ran a hand through his hair, ruffling the front so that a jet black lock fell forward. 'I want to give myself a challenge; not stick with the humdrum.'

'Then write something that will use the full range of her voice.'

'Sounds as if you're suggesting a pop aria!'

'Why not?'

'It's impossible.'

'Then there's your challenge!'

He laughed, but the narrowing of his eyes told her he was assessing her comment. It was a temptation for her to add to it, but sensing he wasn't a man who liked to be pushed, she said no more.

Ahead of her Dick and Sara were walking up the gangplank. Sara caught her heel in a slat of wood and he reached out to steady her, then kept his hand on her waist. Helen turned her eyes away. Sara was no longer a child and must be allowed to live her own life.

Yet though she told herself this, she was still angry. Didn't Dick have enough sense to know he was storing up trouble for himself if he married a girl twenty-five years his junior?

'Anyone for a nightcap?' he questioned as they all reached the deck.

'Bed for me,' Helen said quickly. 'Thanks for a wonderful evening, Dick. I'll see you all in the morning.'

Alone in the air-conditioned tranquillity of her stateroom, she reminded herself yet again that her daughter was free to do as she liked, and that if she couldn't accept Sara's growing closeness to Dick, she must find somewhere else to live.

Feeling inexplicably depressed, and deeply aware that in the not too distant future a decision might be forced on her, Helen went to bed.

A gentle rocking motion penetrated Sara's consciousness and she yawned and opened her eyes, wondering where she was. Memory flooded back as she saw the blue silk tented ceiling above her, and she sat up, plumping her satin-covered pillows, the better to survey her surroundings.

'I could quickly get used to the good life,' she said aloud, pulling a face at her reflection in the mirrored doors behind which lay a vast walk-in wardrobe. She had thought her new apartment luxurious, but it was a slum compared with this!

Her pleasure was dulled by the knowledge that she was sharing her weekend with Benedict, the one man she detested above all others. It was too bad of Dick to have asked him here without telling her. Yet had he done, she would never have come—which was why he'd kept quiet!

How furious she had been when she had come on deck and seen that tall, indolent figure in front of her. It had been all she could do not to walk off the yacht there and then.

Of course Dick knew perfectly well how she felt, but he had invested a great deal of money in her, which he wanted to recoup, and a best-selling album was the quickest way.

So it looked as if she had no choice but to eat humble pie and be charm itself to Benedict, for only then would he deign to lift pen to paper for her.

As she slipped into a black bikini with matching thigh-length jacket which emphasised her shapely legs, she decided it was not only his behaviour to Barbie that made her hackles rise, but his general attitude of superiority; as if he considered himself above human frailty, an aura in no way diminished by his supercilious smile and thick black eyebrows, so often sardonically raised.

Yet why should she concern herself with his feelings towards women, or the world in general? All she was interested in was his music, and she was definitely, but definitely going to be charming to him!

Her decision faltered as she emerged on deck and saw him leaning over the rail, magnificent in the briefest white shorts, his bronzed, well muscled chest partially covered by the sleeves of a white silk sweater casually tied around his neck.

'Sara, so you're an early bird too!' His usually clipped tones were a mocking drawl. 'I thought I'd be having breakfast by myself.'

Remembering her avowal to be nice, Sara swallowed the retort she had been about to make, and was relieved when a steward approached with a salver holding two glasses of fresh pineapple juice.

'English or Continental breakfast?' he asked them.

'Just decaffeinated coffee for me, please,' Sara told him.

'I'll go along with the coffee,' Benedict endorsed, 'but I'll have mine with bacon and eggs, wholemeal toast and marmalade.'

Sara turned away to hide a smile, but his sharp eyes noticed.

'What's so funny?'

'The way you mix health food and heart attack food!'

He laughed. 'I tend to live it up on holiday, but as you see, my conscience won't allow it entirely. But if *you're* so health-conscious, you shouldn't even have decaf.'

'I'm on holiday too! I'll probably even succumb to a croissant with lashings of butter and apricot jam.'

She wandered over to the table and took a chair that gave her a view of Le Touquet. They were moored some quarter of a mile out at sea, the yacht rocking gently on the blue water, like a graceful white bird.

'Do you have a boat?' she asked.

'A small one only. I keep it in California. I have a house in Malibu.'

'Naturally,' she said drily.

'Naturally?'

'It goes with your image.'

'*Your* image of me—which is a strange one.'

'Not strange,' she corrected. 'Simply more realistic than most women.'

His smile was tight. 'I'm thirty-five and more than somewhat successful. Any wonder your fair and phoney sex chase me? They'd think me attractive if I were fat and fifty and resembled a gorilla!'

'Men can be equally false,' Sara said without inflection.

'True.' A silver-covered plate was set before him, and the cover removed to show crisp rashers and two golden-yolked eggs. 'Take you, for example,' Benedict went on as he began eating. 'Your animosity towards me—which I've always thought overly strong, incidentally—either stems from that canary episode, or else is deliberately fabricated to arouse my interest.'

The arrogance of him! Yet even as an angry retort rose to her lips, she saw the logic of his reasoning. Normally she would have accepted his criticism of her singing; even have laughed it off. But his behaviour to Barbie had made it impossible. Still, she had to forget it.

'I've annoyed you, haven't I?' he said.

'Isn't that what you intended? Or do you think I like

being lumped with all the other idiots who chase you?'

His smile showed perfect white teeth, and her anger increased. Was there nothing physical about him she could find to disparage? Even as she tried, her mother joined them.

'Hello, you two, who's drawn first blood?'

'Neither of us,' Sara answered sweetly, glad of a third party to take the heat out of the conversation. 'We're the best of friends.'

'Glad to hear it,' remarked Dick, emerging from his stateroom. 'And what early risers you all are! Usually my guests breakfast in bed.'

'On a glorious day like this?' Helen questioned. 'I'm so full of energy I could scrub the deck!'

'I might hold you to that!'

'How long have you had *Solo*?' asked Sara.

'Three years. It was a present to myself when my company went public. Extravagant of me,' he admitted, 'but what's money for if not to enjoy it?'

'That's a rather hedonistic attitude,' Helen said, then catching Sara's eye, she went scarlet. 'Sorry, Dick—that sounded awfully condemning, and I didn't mean it to be.'

'Forget it,' he said easily.

The soft trill of the telephone called him away, and as he disappeared, Benedict told them, 'For six months every year Dick rents *Solo* and gives the proceeds to the Mayfield Orphanage. But don't let on I told you or he'll have my hide!'

Seeing her mother's embarrassment, Sara gave her a wry look. 'That's the second time you've jumped to the wrong conclusion about Dick!'

'I know.'

'Have I missed out on part of the conversation?' asked Benedict amiably.

'It was an unspoken one,' Helen replied. 'I've a

stereotyped view of what a record producer should be, and Dick keeps proving me wrong!'

'You're not the only one who finds him hard to assess,' Benedict came swiftly to her rescue. 'Publicly he maintains a certain image, but privately he devotes a helluva lot of time to charity.'

'You're making me feel worse and worse!' Helen grimaced. 'I think I'll go bury my head under water! Anyone else for a swim?'

'I'll join you as soon as I've digested my breakfast,' drawled Benedict.

Dropping his napkin, he rose, and Sara's eyes automatically went to his stomach, flat and smooth, the skin as tanned as his chest. As he moved from the table and his shorts dropped an inch lower, she saw there was no paler line of skin to be seen, and imagined him sunbathing nude at his Malibu house. He was good-looking enough to appear in films as well as write musicals for them, she thought, and was mortified to hear herself blurt out:

'Ever thought of being an actor?'

'Only in a nightmare!' His eyes glinted at her, mischief making them more green than grey. 'What provoked the question, Sara? My beautiful body?'

With an aplomb for which she silently applauded herself, she leaned back in her chair and slowly gave him the once-over.

'Actually, yes. You'd make a terrific centrefold for *Cosmopolitan*!'

'I'll bear it in mind if my inspiration runs dry,' he replied, and sauntered away.

'Whatever's got into you, Sara?' her mother hissed. 'Talk about *me* not being a diplomat!'

'I know. But each time I see him I think of Barbie. She hasn't forgotten him, you know. She's still as on edge as a precipice.'

'Making an enemy of Benedict won't help her. And it won't help you either. If you know what's good for your career, you'll——'

'I know. And I was all set to be civil to him too! But I can't seem to help it.'

'Help what?' asked Dick, rejoining them.

'My fear of diving,' Sara lied.

From the corner of her eye she saw Benedict turn from the rail to watch them, and without knowing why, she caught Dick's hand and pressed it to her cheek. It was a childish gesture, but Dick didn't seem to mind, for he knuckled her chin before moving over to pour himself a coffee.

'How about my challenging you two ladies to a game of deck quoits?'

'I'm going to sunbathe,' Helen said.

'Can't say I fancy doing anything energetic just yet,' Sara concurred, watching her mother settle in a deckchair. Her one piece bathing suit, though modest, still showed she had a figure a woman half her age would be proud of, and Sara thought again what a waste it was that her mother was on her own.

'What about a game of Scrabble, then?'

'You're on!'

They played for the best part of an hour, and after Dick had won four times in a row, Sara bowed her head in mock shame and refused to continue.

'Thank God you sing better than you spell,' he teased.

'I even croak better than I spell!'

'And how do you swim?'

'Like an Olympic champion!' Slipping off her jacket, she went towards the steps which had been lowered into the water. 'Come on, Mother,' she called. 'You've been lazy long enough!'

Murmuring agreement, her mother stood up and

followed her. Sara deliberately avoided looking Benedict's way, though she was aware of him jogging the length of the deck, his muscular legs moving with rhythmic grace, his skin shining with perspiration.

Running lightly down the steps to the water, she plunged in. It was icy cold and her breath caught in her throat. But then this was the English Channel, not the Côte d'Azur! There was a splash beside her and she saw Dick had joined them, followed almost at once by Benedict, who made a perfect dive from the topmost step, cleaving the water as smoothly as a hot knife through butter.

For the next half hour they cavorted close to the yacht, not moving too far from it, for though the day was calm there was a slight swell to the sea. Not that it bothered Benedict, who headed strongly towards the shore some half a mile away. Sara wished she could do the same, but was afraid he would think she was following him, so she contented herself with swimming leisurely around.

Her mother was first out of the water, closely followed by Dick, who joined her on the deck.

'I'll stay in a while longer,' called Sara shaking the salt drops from her hair.

'Don't go too far from the boat,' her mother warned, and promising she wouldn't, she swam towards the stern.

Only as she reached it did she roll over on to her back and float, silky tendrils of hair spreading around her.

'Keep swimming, or you'll get cold.'

She recognised the incisive voice, but took no notice of it.

'Are you always so obstinate?' Benedict enquired, 'or do I bring out the worst in you?'

For answer Sara turned over and headed for the steps. Much as she was loath to agree with him, she *was* feeling the cold, and she thought longingly of the towelling coat lying on her chair. Her hand reached for the bottom rung, but before she could touch it a larger tanned one was there first, grasping hers and pulling her round so fast her body jerked hard against his.

The collision robbed the breath from her body, and she gasped and would have slipped back into the water had Benedict not held her fast.

'You're the most bloody aggravating woman I know!' he muttered, bracing himself against the steps, and she had a swift impression of a shiny wet body and crisp black hair sprinkled with droplets, before his head blocked out her vision and his mouth came down on hers.

Sara tried to pull away, but it only served to plunge them deeper into the sea, where the waves buffeted her back against him, and his arms snaked round her to keep her there, body against body, thigh against thigh. So close were they that they seemed indivisible, and she felt the pounding of his heart against her breast, and the whipcord muscles of his legs entwined round hers.

Feeling like a fragile bark fighting the strength of a destroyer, she went limp, hoping to disarm him and escape. But her capitulation only made it easier for him to increase his hold, and his hands moved down her naked back, one to curve upon her waist, the other to press her buttocks tightly against him, so that she felt the hardness of his arousal.

An involuntary tremor shivered through her, and she was aware of her body in a way she had never been before; feeling her breasts swell and tingle, her thighs ache with the desire to part and allow him entry, to clasp him close and urge him to take her.

But it was a flare of desire that lasted only a second, superseded by a deep revulsion against herself as much as against him. Like a wildcat she fought for release, but it only aroused him the more, and the pressure of his mouth intensified, his lips forcing hers apart, his tongue penetrating the moist warmth, darting in and out with gentle stabbing movements that echoed the swelling throb upon her inner thigh.

Desperately she clawed at him, but his kisses were drugging, the ardour of his mouth sending a slow flame rising within her; a flame that quickened into a burning need that brought her arms up round his neck to strain him close, her breasts soft and full upon his rough-haired chest.

'Not an ice maiden after all,' he murmured, unclasping her arms and drawing them down to her sides as he eased himself back on to the top step, then pulled her up beside him.

Sara clutched at the brass rail, her limbs trembling so much she could barely stand. Thoughts ran round in her brain like demons, warning her not to give herself away, not to let him know what a devastating impact he had had on her. Yet how could she hide what was so obvious? Accepting the futility of it, she searched for a way of turning her response into an insult.

'What maiden can remain icy when faced with a Thor?'

'I never saw you thunderstruck,' he said with swift understanding.

'Devastated is more the word,' she replied, forcing a quick smile to lips that were still trembling from the pressure of his. 'You're a sexy man, Benedict, and I'm a normal young woman. I must remember to give you a call if I'm in need of physical release.'

'You mean if your other "friends" let you down?'

'How clever of you to guess,' said Sara sweetly, and plunged back into the water, doing a strong crawl that drew her swiftly away from him.

But not even the water could wash away the waves of shame that engulfed her as she relived her instinctive response to Benedict's touch. It had been an unnerving experience that threatened the very core of her equilibrium, showing her how easy it was to fall prey to sexual appetite; how quickly desire could destroy reason, negating everything one had been brought up to believe.

Yet was it Benedict who was so devastating or herself who was too susceptible? Maybe it was a bit of both. She reached the anchor line and held on to it, letting her body float free as she considered where her thoughts had taken her.

OK, so she'd responded to him. But that only meant she had a normal sexual appetite. Had she not been hindered by an old-fashioned background she would probably have had numerous affairs, but after making such an idiot of herself over Martin, she had found it easier to sublimate her desires to her career.

However, in the past few months this determination had lessened, due in no small part to the different milieu in which she found herself; a milieu where relationships were expendable and sexual favours exchanged as lightly as swansdown. Small wonder some of this attitude had rubbed off on her, eliciting her uninhibited response to a man of experience.

Glancing round, she saw Benedict had gone, and only then did she swim to the steps and climb aboard. To her relief he was not on deck either, and it was lunchtime before he reappeared, clad in brief navy shorts and top, and carrying a book.

'*Great Short Stories of the World*,' her mother read, catching a glimpse of the cover. 'Sounds like required reading for a school exam!'

Chuckling, Benedict accepted a Buck's Fizz from a steward and came to sit beside her, and Sara, a few feet away, regarded him with studied indifference, glad he could not hear the swift beating of her heart, or know how much she longed to slam her fist into his face.

'Not for school,' he answered her mother's remark. 'I'm

simply looking for inspiration for my next libretto.'

'I heard you were toying with the idea of a Pinero comedy,' Dick remarked.

'That was a smokescreen. I'm considering something far more serious.'

'A tragedy? That's pretty daring.'

'I don't see why,' Sara interpolated. 'If they can turn *Les Miserables* into a musical, then anything goes!'

'Hang on, both of you,' said Benedict drily. 'Who said anything about a tragedy? The word I used was "serious".'

'So you did.' Dick's neat features were alive with interest. 'But how serious? I've always felt you should stretch your talent.'

'And have it come twanging back at me?'

'Worried about having a failure? Come on, man, your fame's assured if you have ten flops!'

Grey green eyes slid slowly to Sara. 'What do *you* think?'

'I think talent finds its own level.'

'Would you say yours has sunk or risen since you switched careers?'

'Hey,' Dick intervened, 'that's a pretty nasty question!'

'Benedict's a pretty nasty man,' Sara said dulcetly. 'But he gets away with it because he's so beautiful to look at and lovely to listen to!'

Dick laughed and pulled Sara to her feet. 'I can see Benedict and I will have to keep our serious conversation for when we're alone. What say we have lunch before you start eating each other!'

'Good idea. I'm starving!' Clinging to his arm, Sara let herself be led to the table, and throughout the meal concentrated exclusively on Dick, flirting with him in a way that even surprised herself.

Almost as if he knew there was a deeper reason for her behaviour, he played up to her, and only when lunch was over and Benedict had retired to the far end of the deck to read did he draw Sara aside and ask what was wrong.

'Give me the real reason you're so antagonistic towards him. I don't believe it's because he criticised you when you were in the chorus.'

Acknowledging his right to know, and accepting that she could rely on his discretion, Sara told him about Barbie.

'At last it makes sense to me!' Dick exclaimed when she finished. 'But if your friend's forgiven him, why can't you? I'm not asking you to fall all over him, but if you could bring yourself to be nice ...'

'How nice?'

'Not *that* nice!' Dick said instantly. 'Just friendly enough so he'll write you a couple of songs.'

'Don't you ever give up?' said Sara wryly.

'If I did, I wouldn't be where I am today!'

She lapsed into silence, physically exhausted by her swim, and emotionally wrung out by what had happened in the water.

'You won't mind if I have another go at him, will you, Sara?' Dick enquired, breaking the quiet.

'Not at all.'

'Good.' He hugged her close. 'Hey, you haven't dried out properly! Go and change your swimsuit.'

Nodding, Sara went to her stateroom, wishing she was miles away from Benedict, and that she had never heard his name.

CHAPTER SEVEN

INTENT on keeping her promise to Dick, Sara sought out Benedict later that afternoon as the ship still lay at anchor off Le Touquet. It was a truly glorious day, the sky blue as sapphires, the sea indigo, the yacht a graceful white swan rocking on the water.

Seating herself on the chair next to him, she lay back and raised her face to the sun. If Benedict was surprised she had chosen to sit beside him in preference to her mother, who had positioned herself nearer the bow, he gave no sign of it. In fact he seemed oblivious of everyone, his head bent to his book, his hair shiny as sealskin in the sun.

When fifteen minutes had passed without his speaking, Sara could bear the silence no longer.

'Found a suitable plot?' she asked.

'No.'

She waited for him to elaborate, and when he didn't, she knew he had no intention of making it easy for her.

'If you're interested in doing something serious,' she pushed on determinedly, 'wouldn't it be easier to think in terms of a contemporary situation?'

'Probably.'

Again it was an abrupt answer, and again she brushed it aside. 'If you've always been successful in one genre, it takes courage to try another.'

'You mean you think I don't have any?' He raised his head and looked at her, his eyes unfriendly.

'I wasn't thinking that at all.'

'Then it's the first time you've given me the benefit of the doubt!'

'Yes, well, I——'

'Look, Sara,' he did not wait for her to continue, 'I suppose I owe you an apology for what happened this morning. But you've been provoking me all weekend and I lost my temper.'

'Do you usually sexually assault someone when you lose your temper?' she demanded, forgetting her good intentions yet again.

'Only when the provoker is five foot two, with blonde hair and cat's eyes! And I'd hardly call a kiss a sexual assault.'

'That depends.' She thrust her arm under his nose to show him the ugly bruise on the soft inner skin.

'My God! Did I do that?'

'It wasn't self-inflicted!' she retorted.

'Then I definitely owe you an apology.'

He didn't look in the least contrite—rather that he would be delighted to bruise her all over again—and her promise to Dick waltzed away in the breeze.

'You're an impossible person to be friends with!' she snorted.

'Funny, you've just echoed my thoughts!'

'Then I'll put us both out of our misery,' she snapped, and stalked off to sit beside her mother.

'Shall I tell you something, daughter of mine? I'd never employ you as a company conciliator!'

'I know. But even for Dick's sake I can't pretend to like that—that—swine.'

'Nor for your own sake either! Though I'm rather glad about it.'

'How come?' asked Sara.

'It shows you don't rate success so highly that you're

prepared to put on an act.'

'That may be commendable in *your* eyes, mine, but in Dick's, it makes me a fool!'

'Because he thinks only in terms of monetary success.'

'That's not fair, Mother!' Sara protested. 'He's concerned for me personally.'

'And his investment in you.'

Unexpectedly Dick was beside them, and Sara gave him an extra warm smile in case he had overheard.

'We'll be back in Folkestone by eight-thirty,' he said, ruffling her hair.

'Suits me,' she murmured. 'It's been a fabulous weekend.'

'It certainly has,' her mother echoed, rising. 'I think I'd better go down and pack.'

'We've masses of time,' Sara protested, but her mother was already out of earshot.

'There's something about me that makes your mother keep her distance,' muttered Dick. 'Have I offended her in any way?'

'Of course not. She's still shy of you, I suppose.' Sara pushed back her chair. 'I might as well pack too. I've had enough sun for today.'

Three hours later Sara and her mother were walking across the tarmac of London's Heliport.

Dick was staying aboard the *Solo* a few more days, but Benedict had returned with them and now offered to drive them home. Her mother quickly settled herself in the back of the Ferrari, giving Sara no choice but to sit in front, which she had avoided the last time she had driven with him, when Ella had been in hospital.

He remembered it too, for he asked if she had seen the understudy in the role.

'Not yet,' Sara told him. 'Colin's invited me, but I've been too busy.'

'I thought you two had a thing going?'

'You thought wrong.'

'Bigger fish to fry, eh?' he asked so quietly that only she could hear.

'What's that supposed to mean?'

'That, like most ambitious young women, you can love where it suits you.'

His comment was so outrageous it was all Sara could do not to lash out at him.

'Don't judge me by the women *you* know.' She made a superhuman effort to keep her voice as low as his. 'I've enough confidence in my ability to believe I can make it to the top without selling myself.' There was a whole lot more she could have added, but she was afraid her mother might hear.

The rest of the journey passed in silence, and Sara was glad the lateness of the hour enabled it to be completed quickly. Avoiding Benedict's eyes, she bade him goodnight, noticing sourly that his smile for her mother was surprisingly warm and lit up his face in a way that made him look a stranger compared to the sardonic man she knew.

How topsy-turvy everything was, she thought gloomily as she entered her apartment. Her mother liked Benedict whom she herself loathed, yet did not like Dick, whom she herself admired.

Dick returned to London the following weekend and took Sara to dinner at the Waterside Inn, which had become their favourite eating place during the summer months.

Situated on the Thames, with the windows of the restaurant open to the gentle sound of the lapping river, it gave its clients the impression of dining al fresco, an illusion encouraged by the pink and green décor, and Villeroy Bosch flower-patterned crockery.

As always, he had asked her mother to join them, and had accepted her refusal with an easy smile for which Sara had awarded him top marks.

'The next few times we go out, I don't intend inviting her,' he announced as they sipped a delicious 1980 Bâtard-Montrachet. 'From now on I'm going to play it cool.'

Sara raised her glass to him. 'To coolth!'

He chuckled and drank. 'How's the album coming along?'

'Slowly. Tony and I have short-listed six numbers we'd like you to hear.'

'Do they all have the same theme?'

'Yes. Being single and alone and looking for love—that's a universal theme! I've even thought of a title—"Simply Sara".'

'I like it—yes, very much. And it lends itself to a great sleeve. Just your face on it. Nothing gimmicky or clever, merely a perfectly simple photograph of a perfectly beautiful girl—Simply Sara.'

Her eyes filled with tears and she reached for his hand. 'You say such lovely things to me, Dick.'

'I'm fond of you,' he said gruffly.

'That's an even nicer thing to say!'

For the rest of the meal they talked of everything except music, and only as they drove home through the warm dark night, with Sara's hair lifting in the breeze of motion, did Dick say he wanted an autumn launch for the album.

'We'll record early September, and get cracking right away on the sleeve design and TV commercials,' he told her.

She pulled a face. 'That's the part I hate most. It makes me feel like a packet of detergent!'

'A great idea. How about changing Simply Sara to Soapy Sara?'

She was still smiling at this as she let herself into the apartment, and was half-way across the hall when she saw a note on the table saying Benedict had called. Intrigued, she went towards her mother's bedroom, only stopping as she realised it was well past midnight. Her curiosity would have to wait till morning.

Morning came faster than she liked, for she was woken from sleep to the insistent purr of her bedside telephone. Huskily she answered, shocked into full awareness as she recognised the brusque voice at the other end.

'Sorry if I woke you,' said Benedict, not sounding in the least sorry. 'But I wanted to catch you before you went out.'

Sara glanced at the miniature green and gold enamel clock—a present from Dick—that stood on the table.

'I don't usually go out at six-thirty!' she rejoined tartly, and barely stifled a yawn.

'Had a late night?' he asked, hearing it.

'Not especially.'

'I nearly rang you at the Waterside Inn.'

'Was it that urgent?'

'Damn right it's urgent. A full-scale emergency, in fact. Linda, Ella's understudy, has discovered she's pregnant; and with her history of miscarriages, her doctor's ordered her to bed!'

'How awful for her,' sympathised Sara.

'Awful for us, you mean. We're in trouble unless you can step in.'

'Step in?' she asked, though she knew what he meant.

'Yes. Take over from Linda. You have the voice, and you were in the chorus long enough to know the music. Well, will you do it?'

Heart thumping, Sara drew a deep breath. 'You mean you're asking a canary to come to the rescue?'

'Damn it, woman!' he exploded. 'Were you born a nagger

or did you study for it? What do you want me to do? Go down on my knees and eat dirt? You've got a wonderful voice, Sara, and you know it.'

'Could you put it in writing?'

'I'll write it in my blood if that will satisfy you! Quit playing games with me, will you! I'm offering you the chance of a lifetime and you'd be stupid to turn it down.'

'I *am* stupid,' she cooed. 'I've got a bird brain!'

Gently she replaced the receiver, then waited to feel a thrill of triumph. But all she experienced was a sense of depression, which remained with her even as she rang Tony's doorbell later that morning. They were still finalising the songs for the album, and had three more to choose.

Anne opened the door to her. 'Am I glad to see you! Your agent's rung three times, and you're to call him the minute you get here.'

Knowing the reason for John's agitation, Sara went slowly up to the top floor studio where Tony was already at the piano.

'I suppose I'd better call John before we start work,' she said reluctantly. 'Otherwise he'll interrupt us.'

'With a capital "I", sweetie. He sounded fit to be tied!'

Nervously she dialled his direct line. 'Sara here,' she said as she heard his voice. 'You want me?'

'Only so I can bang your head on the wall! Are you out of your mind, turning down B.P.'s offer?'

'I'm a singer, not a musical comedy actress.'

'Did *My Fair Lady* do Julie Andrews any harm?'

'No, but——'

'Spare me the buts! All the man did was offer you a part in his show—not his hand in marriage! You can't turn it down.'

'Yes, I can,' said Sara firmly.

'Then you'll never be a star,' John came back at her. 'For that, you've got to be determined and dedicated. If you aren't, you shouldn't have signed with Dick. Suffering cats, we're not asking you to make a blue movie! Just to stand in till Ella returns. Think what publicity you'll get. You won the talent contest with a Peters song and now you're helping the great man out. That's even good for a picture in *The Times*!'

'What about my album?' Sara reminded him. 'I'm working flat out on *that*.'

'You'll only have to ease up for a week while you're rehearsing. Then you'll only be tied up evenings and two matinees.'

'Only?' she asked sarcastically. 'Since when are you an advocate of slave labour?'

'Farmers work even longer hours!' countered John. 'Now listen to me, Sara. You've an obligation to accept that part.'

John was echoing what her conscience had been saying to her all morning, and she could no longer fight it. 'Very well, then. I'll call and say I'll do it.'

'No need. Be at the theatre at two this afternoon.'

'Ever thought of being a ventriloquist?' she asked sweetly.

'Why?'

'Because you love speaking for your clients!'

He was still laughing when she hung up.

'John's right,' said Tony by way of comment. 'And there's no sweat with the album. After the way I've trained you, you'll be able to sing these songs in your sleep.'

'It looks as if I may have to! I can't see when else I'll have the time!'

Grinning, he handed her a list of titles. 'Let's run through these, sweetheart, we're still three short.'

For the remainder of the morning they worked together,

Tony playing the arrangement he had already made, Sara singing a bar here and there to see how it fitted her voice. She made several suggestions, all of which he accepted, and they were so immersed they were astonished when Anne came in with coffee and sandwiches and announced that it was one-thirty.

'I'd better munch these in the cab,' Sara exclaimed, grabbing a couple and reaching for her purse. 'I have to be at the theatre in half an hour.'

'You won't get the cane if you're a few minutes late!' Tony teased. 'Don't forget you're doing *them* a favour as well as yourself.'

But all Sara could think of was that she was helping Benedict out of a tight spot, and the thought was like gall.

CHAPTER EIGHT

HAVING spent so many years steeping herself in operatic roles, Sara found playing Daisy a piece of cake.

The most difficult thing she had to tackle was her relationship with Carol, the leading lady, who seemed to regard her as a threat, and did everything she could to ruin her performance, even to the extent of deliberately dropping a large Bible she was holding at a crucial point in Sara's biggest number.

Carol's behaviour was noticed by all the cast, though when Sara tackled Merrit about it, he advised her to forget it.

'But she's so bitchy,' Sara protested, 'and I can't make out why. My role's tiny by comparison with hers.'

'It may be tiny, but you're making the most of it. And that's what's getting up her nose.'

'Well, she's getting up mine,' retorted Sara, and stormed off to the dressing room that had been allocated to her.

If only Ella were well enough to return! But it would be weeks before she did, and Sara was debating whether to have it out with Carol, and try to convince her she didn't have any ambition to play the leading lady, when she heard the American girl speaking directly outside her door, and then the deeper tones of a man.

It took only an instant for her to recognise it was Benedict, and as the voices continued, she realised with dawning discomfiture that neither of them knew she had returned to the dressing room and could hear them.

Should she open the door and casually walk out? Even as she went to, Carol's words rooted her to the spot.

'The only reason I agreed to play Magda was because it was the only way of getting back into your life.'

'And because Magda's a magnificent role,' came Benedict's teasing rejoinder.

'That was a secondary consideration, and you know it. I'm still crazy about you, Benedict, and you can't deny we rang a few bells together.'

'We certainly did!'

He said no more, and the girl's sigh was audible.

'Any other bells ringing for you?' she asked finally.

'A little tinkle now and then. Nothing great.' His tone changed, becoming brisker and more businesslike. 'I've been giving some thought to the second act, and I've decided to put in some extra dialogue for you.'

'That's wonderful! I always felt there wasn't enough interplay between Colin and myself.'

'I'll probably give Sara another number too.'

'I don't see why.' Carol's voice dripped acid.

'That's because you're not the composer, my sweet. But take my word for it that I'm doing what's best for the show.'

Sara tensed, expecting an explosion, but the next thing she heard was Benedict's laugh, and she assumed Carol had pulled a face at him. In any event, when they spoke again their voices were barely audible, and the sound of their footsteps indicated they were moving away.

Later that afternoon Benedict turned up for the matinee, and Sara found him standing in the wings as she came off stage.

'You've settled into the part very well,' he told her.

'The songs aren't difficult.'

'They're not nursery rhymes either!'

Aware of his irritation, she was careful to hide the pleasure she felt at being able to rile him.

'How's the album doing?' he went on.

'Fine—when I can find the time for it!'

'I'll do a couple of numbers for you,' he said laconically. 'As a thank you for helping me out.'

'I'm being paid for it. I didn't take it in order to twist your arm.'

'I'm aware of that. But I'd like to do it. All I need know is the theme, and the full range of your voice.'

Momentarily her eyes met his. 'The theme is being lonely, single, and looking for love.'

'I can't imagine that applying to *you*,' he murmured, then added, 'But I still need to hear you sing.'

'You just have!'

'I mean on my own, so I can jot down any musical phrases I think you do well.' He paused. 'How about forgetting our rough beginning and starting over again?'

Sara shrugged by way of answer, not quite sure what to say.

'How about having dinner with me tonight, if you're free?'

'I'm not.'

'Tomorrow?'

'I'm tied up all week.'

'Then name the day.'

Realising she couldn't refuse, Sara muttered, 'Monday', then spent the entire weekend worrying about it.

But the face she presented to him on Monday evening when he collected her at the stage door was a cool one, as was their conversation as he drove to a discreet little Italian restaurant in Soho. She had expected him to take her somewhere glamorous, and was pleased he had chosen somewhere they could relax and not feel everyone was watching them.

Although this was the first time they had been completely alone together, she found herself surprisingly at ease; hungry too, and she tucked into an aromatic minestrone before doing justice to home-made ravioli, sizzling in a basil-scented sauce.

'I'm glad you don't pick at your food,' Benedict remarked amusedly, eyeing her empty plate. 'For a little thing you can certainly put it away!'

'It's my first meal of the day,' she admitted. 'I'm so nervous until the show's over, I can't look at food.'

'You've no need to be nervous, Sara. You're first rate. Better than Ella, if you must know.'

'I'm only playing it till she's well again, so don't get any ideas.'

'Don't worry, I've no intention of taking the part away from her. But you're so good that . . .' He paused, looking at her reflectively. 'You're giving me the urge to write another musical.'

'I thought you were already planning one—something serious, didn't you say?'

'That's just a foggy idea in my mind—but looking at you has given me a more specific idea. I'd like to write something that will utilise your full range, as well as your acting ability.'

She knew he had paid her the highest compliment possible, and though professionally delighted, she was personally embarrassed, for she didn't want to like this man, didn't want to see him as anything other than an unfeeling swine.

'I know we didn't get off to a good start,' he went on, repeating what he had said a few days ago, 'and if you wish, I'll grovel at your feet to make amends.'

'That won't be necessary.'

'Then what must I do for us to be friends?'

'Why do you want us to be?'

'Why does any man want to be friends with a beautiful girl?'

'Generally to get her into bed!' said Sara so bluntly that he laughed.

'I'm not saying it hasn't crossed my mind, Sara, but it isn't my prime motive.'

'Then what is? I don't believe you're short of girlfriends.'

'I'm curious to see how long you'll intrigue me!' Benedict said with honesty.

'Longer than you'll intrigue *me*. You're the most conceited man I know!'

'It came out that way,' he admitted. 'I'm afraid I put it rather badly. What I should have said was that women generally bore me out of my skull, but for some reason you don't. And I'd like to figure out why.'

'It's because I resist you,' she shrugged. 'If I fell into your lap like a ripe peach, you'd be bored with me too.'

'We'll have to wait and see.'

'You'll wait a long time!'

'I'm noted for my staying power. Part of my success!' he added slyly, and grinned as he saw the colour rush into her cheeks.

Knowing she was blushing, Sara was furious with herself, but fortunately Benedict changed the subject—he knew when to let something rest—and over coffee they talked shop.

It was one o'clock before they left the restaurant, and she rested her head against the back of the car seat. She felt the soft green material of her dress pull slightly, outlining the curve of her breasts, and knew he was eyeing them, though when he spoke his voice was cool.

'I don't know where you live, so you'll have to direct me.'

Within moments they reached a tree-lined turning off the Brompton Road, and he pulled up outside her apartment block.

'A top address for a top singer,' he drawled. 'Lived here long?'

'Three months. Dick found it for me.'

'A year from now you'll be able to afford a mansion.'

'That's not my style,' Sara assured him. 'I prefer to invest my money. Singers never know when their voices will pack up. And in the pop field it's even worse, because you can fall out of public favour.'

'You can always marry!'

'I don't regard a husband as a meal ticket,' Sara said coldly.

'That's what all women say—till they've got the ring on!'

Silently Sara stepped from the car, but as she reached the glass entrance door, she found Benedict beside her, his mouth curved in a smile.

'What's the joke?' she asked.

'I was thinking how cool we're playing it. Like a couple of Neil Simon characters.'

'The characters *you* write about are pretty cool too.'

'But deep down they have heart—like me!'

Unable to restrain a disbelieving sniff, Sara walked into the lobby.

'Don't you believe I have a heart?' Benedict asked, following her in.

'Everyone has. Only yours is encased in ego!'

For answer he caught her with sudden swiftness and pressed his mouth on hers.

She did not resist him, nor did she respond, and even when he rubbed his lips backwards and forwards across her soft ones, she remained passive.

'At least you haven't smacked my face,' he said, drawing away from her.

'I'm saving that for another time.'

'You think there will be?'

'I'm sure of it. The more successful the Casanova, the harder he finds it to accept that anyone can resist him!'

'Upon which comment, lovely Sara, I'll bid you goodnight and live to fight another day!'

Trembling, she turned her back on him and stalked into

the lift. What a nerve he had, asking if they could be friends and then making it clear he saw her primarily as a sex object!

Was that why he had offered to write a musical for her? To soften her up for the kill? Well, he had another think coming. If he was the last man on earth she wouldn't go to bed with him.

Sara was amused that Benedict did not get in touch with her again. She had obviously convinced him he'd have no luck bedding her, and had decided to cut his losses. After all, why bother with the difficult when the easy was so available!

It was Carol who eventually told her he had gone to New York, and Sara used his absence to invite Barbie to see her play Daisy, astonished to learn her friend already had.

'Why didn't you come backstage!' she exclaimed. 'Anyway, you should have asked me for a ticket.'

'I can afford to buy one—my flower business is improving, and to prove it, this lunch is on me!'

It was Wednesday and matinee day, and Barbie had suggested they meet for a gossip at a small restaurant round the corner from the theatre.

'You've lost weight since I last saw you,' her friend went on. 'Anything worrying you? I've never seen you so thin.'

'I'm thin because I'm working like a dog,' Sara told her. 'Seven performances a week plus slogging away with Tony.'

'Is your Mr Cawthorne trying to kill the goose that's laying his golden eggs?'

'I haven't laid *one* yet!'

'You will. Dozens of them!'

'I hope so.'

Sara picked up the menu, at the same time watching Barbie surreptitiously. She was almost her old self again;

jaunty in a scarlet suit, her conversation more animated, with no mention of the past, other than that her divorce would be final in six weeks.

'Until then I'm lying low,' Barbie added. 'All I need is for Alex to find me doing something I shouldn't! He's not above a spot of blackmail.'

'You've never done anything you shouldn't,' Sara said firmly, and only as she saw Barbie avoid her eyes did she realise she and Benedict must have been lovers. The thought filled her with irrational anger, and she pushed it away.

'I suppose you see quite a bit of Benedict,' Barbie broke the silence. 'You haven't mentioned him, so I assume you're being your usual diplomatic and misguided self!'

'Misguided?' queried Sara.

'Well, I've told you again and again I don't mind talking about him.'

'Well, I do! So let's consign him to the past and talk about the future. What are your plans?'

'To remarry as soon as I can.'

Sara was stunned. Surely Barbie wasn't harbouring hopes of resurrecting her romance?

'Anyone I know?' she questioned.

'No. I was—er—just using a figure of speech. What I meant is that I'd like to, eventually.'

The answer, though wordy, lacked conviction, and Sara was still puzzling over it when Dick came into the dressing room later that night to take her to supper.

'Would you mind awfully if I went home? I'm sorry, Dick, but I'm always bushed after a matinee day.'

'I'm the one who should apologise. It was stupid of me not to realise. Home it shall be. But if you'd like to go somewhere first for a snack ...'

'Mother always leaves me a thermos of hot chocolate and sandwiches. You can share them if you like.'

'That's the best offer I've had in weeks!'

'You've only yourself to blame,' Sara smiled. 'It's ages since you've been to the apartment.'

'You told me to play it cool, remember?'

'Not ice-cold, though!'

His face fell. 'I seem to be doing everything wrong where your mother's concerned. In business I can feign with the best of 'em, but I loathe playing games in my personal life. You've surely guessed by now how I feel about her?'

'I'd be daft if I didn't,' smiled Sara.

'So how shall I proceed?'

'By doing what comes naturally to you!'

'Now *that* I understand!'

As Sara let herself and Dick into the apartment, her mother came out of the living-room to greet her, glowing from her bath and wrapped in a peach satin housecoat—Sara's birthday present to her last week.

'Look who's come back with me,' Sara said cheerily, moving aside for Dick to step forward.

Startled, her mother hurriedly buttoned the top of her housecoat. 'I'm sorry, I wasn't expecting anyone,' she stammered.

'Dick's not anyone. He's a friend.' Sara took in the thermos and the sandwiches on a side table. 'I thought we'd have a snack here.'

'I'm sure Dick doesn't like hot chocolate!' her mother said quickly.

'Too right!' he chuckled. 'I'm a coffee man. I'll come into the kitchen and help you make it.'

'You certainly won't. It will only take me a minute.'

Helen almost ran from the room, and Dick flung Sara a wry look which said 'what now?' to which she responded with an equally wry one. But the instant she heard her mother's step in the hall, she flopped on to the settee and closed her eyes.

'Darling, what's wrong?' Helen James asked as she came in.

'The beginning of a migraine, I think.'

'Go to bed,' said Dick at once, catching on with commendable insight. 'I'm sure your mother won't mind entertaining me while I have my coffee.'

Hiding a smile, Sara went languidly out, and in the hall did a little jig before going to her room.

Although not tired enough to sleep, she went to bed and turned out the light in case her mother peeped in to see how she was. She twisted and turned restlessly for a long while, thinking of Barbie and hoping her friend wouldn't fall for another rotter.

She must have dozed eventually, for she awoke with a start as the front door clicked shut. Glancing at her clock, she saw it was past two. Dick must have drunk the pot dry! Happily she snuggled back on her pillows.

In the morning her mother awoke her with breakfast in bed, and Sara yawned prodigiously and protested she was being spoiled.

'You're always off colour after a migraine,' came the answer.

'I feel fine now.' Sara sipped her orange juice. 'Did Dick stay long?'

'I couldn't get rid of him till two,' her mother told her.

'You must have been good company!'

'He was probably hoping you'd feel better and come back.'

'I doubt it. Don't put yourself down, Mother.'

'I'm not. But Dick's *your* friend, not mine.'

'I'm sure he'd like to be yours too. I think——' The telephone cut her short, and Sara picked it up, smiling as she recognised Dick's voice. 'We were just talking about you! What? Yes, I'll tell her. On second thoughts, do so yourself.' Sara held out the phone, but her mother was already half out the room, muttering that she had an appointment.

'Sorry, Dick, she's gone out,' whispered Sara as the door closed. 'How did it really go?'

'One step forward and two back! She's one very scared lady. Do you think I should ask her out to dinner on her own? I know she's refused before, but——'

'Nothing ventured, nothing gained!'

'How true. And *you* may still get your two songs. Benedict's back from the States and has invited us to lunch on Sunday.'

'That's my one day of rest.' Sara was chagrined the invitation had not come to her direct. 'I suppose I have to go?'

'You suppose right. And no pretended migraine either!'

On Sunday Sara dressed with care, taking care to make it look as though she hadn't!

Her pleated crêpe-de-chine dress was in her favourite almond green, and she wore only lipstick and mascara. Her hair had grown—it needed trimming, but she was working too hard to find any spare time—and it fell in a thick bell to her shoulders, with several fronds curling forward giving her a slightly dishevelled, sensual air.

It was her first visit to Benedict's home, and anticipating the rampantly modern, she was agreeably surprised to find a two-storey, double-fronted Regency house set in a quiet backwater in Kensington.

The entrance hall was the last word in elegant simplicity: black and white tiled floor, crimson-carpeted stairs curving gracefully to the upper storey, where a tall window was draped with crimson and black taffeta, the colour repeated in the Chinese vases on the marquetry table by the front door.

To her right she glimpsed what she assumed to be the

library—booklined, with a mahogany sofa table covered
with neat piles of paper—and several easy chairs on the
glowing Persian carpet. To her left, double doors led into
an immense living room that ran the full depth of the house.

Some forty people were milling around there: at the
white and gold grand piano that stood in one corner; in
front of the graceful Adam fireplace where multi-coloured
begonias lit the room in place of coal; lounging on cream
suede settees, puffy as clouds; or strolling around the wide
York stone terrace at the far end, where blue and white
striped hammocks and garden chairs overlooked a magnificent flower-filled garden that appeared to roll on for ever.

Sara recognised several of the cast, and was pleased to see
Ella, hospital-pale and clinging to a solicitous Colin. At the
sight of Sara he waved a hand self-consciously but made no
move to come over, which delighted her.

As she followed Dick further into the room, with
'darlings' and 'angels' wafting around them, she saw no
sign of her host. Only as she turned to accept a glass of
champagne from a manservant did she glimpse his broad-
shouldered frame on the terrace, chatting up a dramatic-
looking redhead who was almost wearing a low-cut white
dress. Trust him!

Quickly she smiled at Dick, reassured by his solid
presence, and was talking to him with forced animation
when Benedict joined them.

'Glad you could make it, Dick.' His glittering eyes glided
over Sara. 'You're looking very fetching.'

'Dick likes me in green.'

'Do you always please the men you know?' he murmured
as Dick turned to say hello to someone else.

'If they mean something to me, yes.'

'Would you wear red for *me*?'

'I'd wear nothing for you,' she retorted.

'That's better still!'

Her face flamed. 'That wasn't what I meant.'

'Too bad. You've missed out on a great experience.'

'Why, you conceited . . .'

With an enormous effort Sara swallowed the rest of her retort as Dick swung their way again, and had to content herself with giving him a frozen look. He returned it with one of sardonic amusement, his raised eyebrows signifying that had they been alone, she would have received the sharp edge of his tongue. As it was he acted the perfect host, seeing their drinks were replenished and introducing them around before he finally went back to the terrace.

Barry Dent, a well-known disc jockey, came over to chat to Dick, and Sara let her mind wander until her attention was caught by Dick saying he was delaying her album.

The instant they were alone, she rounded on him. 'What's the reason for it? And how is it I'm the last to know?'

'Tony and I only decided this morning. He thinks you're under too much pressure to complete it any earlier, and I agreed with him.'

Her relief at the breathing space was soured by the knowledge that Benedict would think the postponement a ploy to give him time to produce some songs for her, and she'd have liked nothing better than to say that if the matter was left to her, she'd as soon sing hymns!

She was still feeling irritated by the deal when she went out to the terrace for lunch. Small tables had been set all the way along it, and as the guests took their places, a bevy of waitresses emerged with trays of mouthwatering food. There was a choice of excellent wines, and champagne flowed like water, except that the water itself was expensive Malvern! Sara drank sparingly, though, a genuine headache threatening. But then Benedict always gave her a pain in the neck!

As if he knew it, he caught her eye and winked, and she quickly looked down at her plate, concentrating on her poached salmon as if it were a slice of gold! When next she looked up he was still watching her, his chair at the next table placing her in his direct line of vision. The redhead was one side of him, the disc jockey the other, and something in Benedict's face told her he had just learned the new date for the album.

If I'd been nice to him when he took me out to dinner, he'd have written those songs already, fumed Sara, slitting her brandied peach as if it were his throat. Damn Benedict Peters!

Lunch over, Dick was commandeered by Carol, and Sara strolled into the living room to escape the sun. Sinking on to a settee, she wondered how soon she could decently leave.

'Both your men deserted you?' She tilted her head to see the man of her nightmares beside her.

'I'm perfectly happy on my own.'

'You don't look it.' He sat next to her, his body indolent as he stretched his long legs in front of him. 'In fact you look decidedly jaded.'

'That's hardly surprising,' she sighed. 'I'm exhausted!'

'Ella should soon be well enough to take over from you.'

'That's the best news I've had in weeks!'

Sara did not look at him. But she felt his eyes on her and tried to still her trembling body. Amazing how disliking someone could make you weak at the knees!

'About those songs I promised you,' he went on. 'If you'll come——'

'I won't come anywhere with you!' she flared. 'If that's the price I have to pay, you can keep your music!'

Without a word he rose and left her, and mortified by her loss of temper—which had shown him how hurt she was—

she decided to leave a note for Dick saying she was going home.

As she stood up, soft chords echoed in the room, and she saw that Benedict had seated himself at the piano. His profile was turned towards her and she could not help thinking how distinguished he looked with his fine cut mouth, patrician nose, and glossy black hair curving into the nape of his neck.

He started playing a medley of his compositions, moving effortlessly from one hit to another. And how many there were! The sounds around him stilled: glasses no longer tinkled, conversation ceased, and one by one everybody left the terrace and tiptoed back into the room.

Someone softly began to hum, and Benedict took up the refrain, his voice a melodic, untrained baritone, yet with a natural rhythm that cleverly illumined his brilliant lyrics. Lyrics of joy and sadness, of man's faithlessness and woman's longing.

Young couples smiled at one another and thought of the future, older ones sighed, remembering the past. Was there anything this man couldn't do? Sara wondered wryly, and knew that like him or not, she could not decry his talent.

There was another ripple of chords, and this time the plaintive melody and lyrics were new as he sang of a lost love. The song that followed, which she also didn't recognise, was the exact opposite: a joyful piece of love found again, that set hands moving to its beat; a movement that turned into sustained applause as, with a sweep of chords, Benedict finally withdrew his fingers from the keyboard.

'I see you haven't lost your touch, darling.' Carol was the first to congratulate him, her full-breasted body draped over the piano. 'I thought you weren't writing pop any more?'

'These are my "thank you" to Sara for standing in for

Ella.' He rose and strolled across to her. 'I hope you like them?'

'I—er—oh, very much,' she stammered, embarrassed and angry with herself. If only she hadn't lost her temper with him earlier!

'When you turned down my invitation just now,' he said softly, 'I was only going to ask you to come over to the piano while I played for you.'

'I know. I behaved like a fool. Please forgive me.'

'Only if you take a stroll with me in the garden.'

There was no way she could refuse, nor pull her hand free from his as he clasped it and drew her outside. Swiftly he led her across the terrace and down shallow stone steps to a long, rose-covered pergola perfumed with a thousand scents, at whose apex stood a wrought iron and glass gazebo, filled with trailing plants and flowers.

Not until they were inside and he had closed the door did he release her hand.

'You suit this interior,' he said deeply, his eyes roaming over her face and body. 'With your amber hair and that flowing dress, you're a pre-Raphaelite painting come to life.'

'I wouldn't fancy one on my wall! But thanks for the compliment.'

He laughed. 'You're never at a loss, are you?'

'I *am* at the moment.' Sara drew a painful breath. 'I really am sorry I was rude to you before.'

'Forget it. I have.'

His gaze remained intent on her, and she turned away quickly to study the elegant symmetry of the house, its tall, narrow windows marked by white shutters.

'My bedroom's the one with the balcony,' he said. 'On sunny mornings I breakfast there.'

'You have a lovely view.'

'Particularly now.'

He leaned against the glass wall, arms folded across his chest as he went on watching her. In the small space he loomed large, his silk knit shirt clinging to his broad shoulders as tightly as his cream pants to his muscular thighs. One man to have so much! Looks, charisma, fame. If only he had a heart to go with it!

'Why the frown, Sara? Am I still your enemy?'

'Of course not.'

'But you don't regard me as a friend, though. I wish I knew what I'd done to rouse your enmity.'

'Does it matter? Or does every woman have to fall at your feet?'

'Not fall,' he replied wryly. 'But I don't appreciate her looking as if she'd enjoy stamping on them! Be honest with me, Sara, and tell me what you've got against me. You've fobbed me off long enough.'

She agreed with him, and moving a step further away from him, took another deep breath. 'Barbie Lomax is my best friend. And anyone who hurts her hurts me.'

'Barbie Lomax?'

He looked puzzled, and Sara could have sworn he didn't know who or what she was talking about. Her anger intensified and she could cheerfully have hit him. How could he forget the girl he'd been going to marry?

'Barbie,' he repeated slowly, and all at once his eyes narrowed and he let out a sigh. 'So that's it! Now it's beginning to make sense.' His gaze sharpened. 'What did she say to you about me?'

'What do you think?'

'Nothing good, I imagine.'

'How wrong you are! Even though you behaved disgustingly, she actually defends you! My God, when I think of it . . . That she was only in hospital because of *you*!

'If Barbie isn't angry with me, why should you be?'

'Because I'm not in love with you and can see you for the

swine you are! How could you leave her the way you did?'

'I wasn't in love with her,' he shrugged.

Sara raged at his insouciant reply. 'Then why did you pretend you were? Or promise to marry her? If you were only interested in an affair, couldn't you have found someone in your own league—not a girl already hurt by a rotten marriage?'

'Don't blame me for her marriage, Sara. Though you obviously blame me for everything else!'

'Damn right I do!'

'I did what I thought best,' he stated.

'Best for you! That's all you care about.'

'Not quite.' His hand snaked out and pulled her close, his eyes ice-grey with anger. 'I don't believe in letting people live in cloud cuckoo land. If I change my mind about something or someone, I don't hide it. I find that's the best way. And according to what you've just said about Barbie, she agrees with me!'

'Because she's a fool!'

'You mean she's more understanding than you are.'

'How you twist everything to suit yourself,' Sara choked. 'I hate you—everything about you!'

'Then why sing my songs?'

'Because Dick wants me to.'

'Rubbish! You didn't even know him when you entered the talent contest.'

'It was Tony who chose——'

'Stop hiding behind other people, Sara. You suit yourself—same as you say I do! As I'm going to do now.'

With a movement so swift and strong she had no chance to escape it, he pulled her tight against him. The violence of his embrace told her he had gone beyond reason, and she wished she had been less vehement in her attack. Besides, Barbie wouldn't thank her for it!

'Let me go,' she said coldly, refusing to struggle.

'Not yet.' Benedict's head lowered to hers and his voice thickened. 'Forget Barbie. She's the past and you're the present.' His breath was warm against her skin, and his tongue ran lightly across her lower lip. 'Doesn't it give you a thrill to know the famous Benedict Peters longs to take you to bed? Wants to undress you and kiss every inch of your tantalising body?'

'Thrill?' Sara choked. 'It makes me sick!'

'That's what your lips say,' he murmured, pressing her hips so tightly against his that she could feel the swelling, pulsating throb of him. 'But your body says something different; that my touch excites you so much you don't want me to stop.'

'You're mad!' she gasped.

Only now did she begin to struggle, frightened by his cold calculation. They were out of sight of the terrace and no one could see them. The pergola was deserted, and dance music coming from the living room told her no one would venture this far.

'Let go of me,' she reiterated, trying to push him away.

'Not yet. Kiss me first, Sara, hold me. Don't pretend you're indifferent, because I know you aren't. From the moment we met, we both knew it would end like this. You fancy me as much as I fancy you, and you hate yourself for it.'

How clever of him to have guessed! Yet why shouldn't he? Nearly every woman he met reacted the same way! Resisting her desire for him, she made a superhuman effort to sound amused.

'If you could market your sex appeal, Benedict, you'd be a billionaire! And you're right about me hating myself. Fancying you is a mindless desire that puts me in the same category as a bitch in season!'

He gave a sharp intake of breath. 'And a bitch is what you are! No, I take that back. You're a vixen—sharp and vicious—but I love you for it. So insult me as much as you like, Sara. It arouses me even more than your touch!'

Sickened that her jibes should give him pleasure, she knew an overwhelming urge to hurt him physically. Her hands came up to rake his face, but he was too quick for her. Even as her fingers touched his cheek, he grabbed them and wrenched them down to her sides, laughing at her impotent fury.

'Don't stop,' he crooned. 'Keep playing hard to get, my lovely Sara. It will make your capitulation all the more exciting!'

Roughly he gripped her hair and jerked her head back until her mouth was directly beneath his. He gave another sharp tug, and as her lips parted in a cry of pain, his own came down to stifle it—hard and punishing in its fierceness.

It was a kiss without a vestige of tenderness, and the more Sara struggled the more ruthless it became. His hands roamed her body, hard as his mouth, awakening sensations she tried in vain to resist. How could her breasts not swell to the rough urgency of his grasp, her nipples not rise to the insistent rub of his fingers? It sent fire coursing through her veins and tremors through her limbs. Her knees went weak, her whole being overcome by a wave of passion so strong that she felt herself drowning in it.

But Benedict was insensitive to her feelings. It was his own he cared about; his determination to show he was her master superseding all else. 'I'm the one in control,' his touch seemed to say, 'and I'll take you when I want and leave you when I want, just as I do all the women in my life!'

'Beautiful Sara,' he muttered against her mouth. 'You taste of honey, but your words are acid.'

He let go of her so abruptly that she staggered, saved from falling by the plant-covered wall behind her. A sharp thorn dug into her flesh, but she was immune to its rasp, aware only of the man in front of her. All trace of anger had gone from him, and he was once again the urbane, controlled host she had met earlier that day.

'Well, Sara,' he said gently, slipping one hand into the pocket of his jacket, and looking so casual it was hard to believe that only seconds ago he had acted like one possessed. 'Now I've shown you how correct your assessment of me is, you'll be able to sleep easy!'

'Easy in the knowledge that your leaving Barbie was the best thing that happened to her!'

'I'll know where to come if I need a character reference!'

'How can you be so unfeeling?' she cried.

'I don't have any feelings—other than purely sexual ones!'

Sara swallowed hard. 'I won't stay in your show—I couldn't! I'll ask Merrit to let my understudy take over.'

'The hell you will! You'll play Daisy till Ella gets back.'

'I won't!'

'You will. Walk out on me, and I'll make sure you never work in the theatre again.'

'I couldn't care less! I'm a singer, Benedict. I don't need the theatre.'

'Dick wouldn't agree with you.'

Reference to Dick lessened Sara's vehemence, though not her anger. 'You can't still *want* me in your show?' she gasped.

'I don't. But I never allow personal feelings to dictate my professional ones.' Benedict motioned her to precede him from the gazebo. 'And to prove it, I won't even take back the two numbers I wrote for you. You see, Sara, that's how little I care what you think of me.'

The arrogance of the man! She'd rather die than sing them. Yet as the thought came, she knew she'd ignore it. Benedict was right, she admitted despondently: she was as expedient as he. The knowledge was like a physical blow, and she felt too sickened by it to move.

'I w-won't come back to the house for the moment,' she said huskily.

'Shall I send Dick out?'

'No, thanks. I'd like to be alone.'

'With such a sweet disposition and so tolerant an outlook,' he murmured, 'you should be used to it.'

Sara turned away quickly to hide her tears. She had no idea why she felt so shattered; all she knew was that she had derived no satisfaction from letting Benedict know what she thought of him. Indeed, it had served only to make him her enemy. Yet that wasn't true, for he had made it abundantly clear he was indifferent to her—which was even more galling.

Once again she realised how ambivalent her reactions were to him. To begin with she had damned him for what he had done to Barbie. Now it was his behaviour to herself which hurt; hurt so much that she was scared to analyse why.

Soberly she looked out across the lawn, reminding herself that Benedict wasn't worth hating, any more than he was worth loving. He might be a brilliant composer, but on the human level he was non-existent!

CHAPTER NINE

IN THE days that followed, Sara regretted the tirade she had let loose on Benedict, and wondered what would have transpired between them had there been no Barbie on the scene. A love affair, that was for sure! Yet it would only have brought her momentary pleasure, for she was not cut out to be one of legion!

The highlight of her week was Tony's pleasure in her two songs, and he said he would like a couple of weeks to do the arrangements before rehearsing them with her.

'Now Dick's postponed the launch date, there's no need for us to break our backs,' he explained.

'Thank heaven for small mercies!' Sara answered with relief, hoping that by then Ella might have returned to the show, leaving her free to exit from Benedict's world.

Not that she could fault his behaviour on the few occasions when they had met backstage, for he had been unfailingly polite, even to the extent of chatting to her—though his eyes had remained blank as an empty page.

Shortly after that disastrous lunch party, Merrit had called an extra rehearsal, and Benedict, lean and saturnine in black slacks and sweater, announced that he had written in another song in the second act, in place of a dance sequence.

'Great!' exclaimed Carol. 'I always thought all that hoofing slowed down the action.'

'The audience don't think so,' the choreographer snapped.

Carol ignored her. 'Give me the song, Benedict, and we'll run through it.'

'I'll play it first.'

Seating himself at the piano, he began to do so, but half-way through Carol interrupted him angrily.

'That song's for Daisy!'

He nodded and went on playing.

'I'm the star,' Carol persisted, her voice rising, 'and it's *me* the audience pay to hear!'

'They hear you eighty per cent of the time,' he drawled, and ignoring her angry exclamation, motioned Sara to come and take the song sheet he was holding out. 'Merrit will rehearse this with you. I'd like it to go in as soon as possible.'

'Must I interpret it as you did?' she asked.

'No, I'll leave it to you. You've got excellent judgement of a song.' He added so quietly that only she could hear, 'It's only poor when it comes to men!'

Her eyes flashed but she said nothing, refusing to be needled into an answer she might regret.

Adding a song and removing a dance sequence meant more rehearsals, and the cast worked like Trojans for several days. Everyone except Carol agreed it was an improvement, as did the audience on the Thursday night, when they gave Sara a rapturous reception.

Coming off stage as the American star went on, she knew she had made an enemy; not unusual in a profession where egos were large and easily bruised.

Her only disappointment was that Benedict wasn't there to witness her success, for he had unexpectedly flown to the States that very morning, and though Merrit said he'd be sending him the reviews, Sara would have enjoyed seeing his face as the audience had shouted their appreciation of her.

She had to wait two weeks before she did, returning to the wings after her ovation to find him standing there. Tanned deep bronze, he was more devastating than ever, and she guessed he had been in California rather than New York.

Politely he moved aside to let her pass, but she remained in front of him, nerving herself for what she wanted to say.

'I'd like to—to thank you for giving me that song, Benedict. It's an absolute winner.'

'So I've been told.' His voice, like his manner, was noncommittal.

'After the things I said to you, I didn't—I didn't——' Sara stopped, embarrassed, and before she could continue, he laughed without amusement.

'Don't tell me you're apologising, Sara?'

'Not for what I actually said.' His sarcasm revived her animosity. 'But as a guest in your home I shouldn't have said it.'

'I must remember to invite you back next time we've something to discuss! It's obviously the only way of curbing your tongue!' He turned away from her, then paused. 'If it makes you happier—I know how much it riles you to feel grateful to me—I didn't write that number with you in mind. It's Daisy's song and you happen to be playing her.'

Knowing she had been given her come-uppance by a master, Sara stalked off, but hardly had she gone a few steps when he was in front of her.

'Wait—I haven't finished. I'm the one who should apologise now. It's stupid for us to keep sniping at each other. The cast are beginning to notice, and once they start gossiping, it'll be fodder for the newshounds. I know how close you are to Barbie, but what you don't seem to realise is that personal relationships can't be judged by outsiders. So I suggest we put the whole thing behind us and be civil to each other.'

What he said made sense, and Sara nodded acceptance of the olive branch. Benedict regarded her for a long moment, his expression inscrutable, then strode back to the wings.

'What were you and Benedict talking about?' Colin had come up unnoticed.

'Just idle chat.'

'It seemed more intimate than that.'

Colin's tone was brotherly rather than loverly, and Sara momentarily rested against him.

'We've decided to call an armed truce,' she told him.

'Thank the lord for that! A man like Benedict could hurt you.'

'I've more sense than to fall for him.'

'Since when did sense have anything to do with love—or sex?'

'I want neither from him.' Luckily she heard her cue just then, and hurried off.

At the end of the show there were groans of disappointment from everyone on hearing another rehearsal had been called for the following morning to work on a song Benedict had written for Carol. No one could accuse him of not being a diplomat, Sara thought. But then Carol was going to be playing the lead on Broadway and he had to be.

'May I cry off?' she asked Merrit. 'Tony's booked a recording session at the studio and——'

'Absolutely not! Carol's song follows on from yours and it's important you get the timing right. But with luck, you should be free by midday.'

Early next morning Sara's alarm catapulted her into consciousness. Yawning with fatigue, she showered and went into the kitchen to make herself some toast.

She was eating it when the telephone rang, and a young man called Bill Jenkins from Photo Syndication told her she was to cut rehearsal and go to Osterley Park.

'What for?' she asked.

'Some publicity shots. It's a National Trust house and will make a nice background.'

'How do I get there?'

'Take the subway to Osterley, and a cab from there.'

'Who else is going apart from me?' asked Sara hoping she could cadge a lift from Colin.

'Search me. I was only told to contact you and tell you to be there at ten.'

The moment he hung up, she dialled Colin. Getting no reply, she deduced he had left for the theatre. Anyway, if he'd been asked to the photo session he would have checked to see if she had been called too.

Hurriedly she changed into one of her prettiest dresses, then to be on the safe side, put two others into a small holdall before dashing in to let her mother know where she was going.

Although barely nine, it was already scorchingly hot; one of those Indian Summer days that made it impossible to envisage the approach of winter. Unwilling to arrive at Osterley looking as if she had crossed the Sahara, Sara hailed a passing cab. The journey was outside the city limits, but she was in no mood to quibble about the cost.

Arriving at the beautiful Adam house with time to spare, she was surprised to see so few cars. Still, better early than late, she thought as she paid off the cabby.

There was no sign of a photographer either, and deciding everyone was inside, she climbed the wide sweep of stone steps and crossed the paved court into a magnificent hall with an intricately designed marble floor. This was empty too, as were all the reception rooms, and she began to feel like a ghost in search of a place to haunt!

Surely everyone couldn't have come and gone? Hurriedly she went in search of a guard.

'Photographic session?' he echoed her question, scratching his chin. 'I haven't heard of one, and I'd be bound to know.'

'May I use your phone to call the theatre?' she asked. 'If I've made a mistake, they'll put me right.'

Minutes later Sara set down the receiver, totally mystified. No one knew anything about a photo session and Benedict and Merrit were furious that she wasn't at rehearsal.

On the journey back to the West End, Sara realised she had been the victim of a hoax. The perpetrator instantly sprang to mind, and as she walked into the theatre and heard Carol belting out the very song Benedict had written for herself two weeks ago, her suspicions hardened.

Without thought, she hurried down to the front row of the stalls where he was sitting.

'Thanks for coming,' he said tightly, thin-lipped with anger. 'I hope it didn't inconvenience you!'

'I'm sorry,' she whispered back, 'but——'

'You damn well aren't! You'd no intention of coming. I heard you ask Merrit to let you off.'

Furious that he wouldn't let her explain, Sara jumped up. As she did there was a loud crash, and she swung round to see Carol sprawled at her leading man's feet, her body half covered by a massive piece of sky scenery.

'My God!' Benedict leapt on stage, and with Colin and Merrit carefully lifted the canvas and plywood off the unconscious girl.

Someone raced to phone for an ambulance, and the cast stood by silently, frozen with shock.

'If she'd been standing six inches further to the left,' said Colin, 'she'd have taken the full force of it and been killed.'

Sara's eyes moved the few feet, and she shuddered. 'That's where *I* always stand when I sing that number!'

'Then you can thank your lucky stars you were late!'

Or thank Carol, Sara thought, trying not to think in terms of retribution as she watched the star being lifted on to a stretcher and borne away, Benedict at her side.

Merrit rubbed hand across the top of his head, and said to no one in particular, '*Now* what the hell do we do?'

'Call in the understudy,' someone said.

'She was stung by a wasp yesterday, and her face is puffed like a bullfrog's!'

It's as if gremlins have taken over the show, thought Sara. First Ella, then Carol, now a wasp!

'Break for lunch, everyone,' Merrit called wearily. 'We'll resume at two. By then we should have news of Carol.'

They all adjourned to the local pub for a lunch they were too worried to eat, and returning to the theatre, heard the bad news that Carol had broken her collarbone and would be out of action for six weeks.

'Lucy's been given an antihistamine injection,' Merrit went on to say, 'so luckily she can take over tonight. But she isn't good enough to do it till Carol returns, though she'll hold the fort until we find someone else.'

At least it was a reprieve, Sara thought, though watching Benedict, who had come in while Merrit was talking, she noticed how pale he was beneath his tan, and guessed he did not ride the various crises as easily as he made out.

For the next week Lucy did a valiant job. But at best she was a shadow of the star, and the cast were on tenterhooks wondering who was going to replace her.

Sara was the first to find out. Going into her dressing room on Saturday evening, she found Benedict there. Her dresser was nowhere to be seen, and even as she glanced round he said:

'I told Ada to get lost for a while. I want to talk to you.'

'Is Ella coming back sooner than you thought?' Sara asked instantly.

'No. This has nothing to do with Ella. It's Carol. She won't be returning to the London show. The break to her collarbone's worse than we thought, and by the time she's fit, she'll have to open on Broadway. So that leaves you.'

'Leaves me where?'

'Taking over her role.'

'You must be joking!' exclaimed Sara.

'It's no joking matter. It's the obvious solution and I don't know why I didn't think of it before. With the right coaching you'll do fine.'

'Spare me the soft soap!' she said sarcastically.

'It isn't. I mean it. You're exactly right for the part. I

know you never liked the way Carol played it, and now you'll have a chance to do it *your* way.'

'I don't want the chance, thank you! I can manage Daisy fine, but Magda's an enormous role and I can't do it.'

'You can.'

'No,' she insisted.

'Yes, Sara.'

Feeling the ground being cut from under her, she searched for another excuse. 'Ella isn't fit enough to come back yet, so who'd take over from *me?*'

'Sheena Roberts. She'll be playing Daisy on Broadway, and she's agreed to come here till then.' Benedict moved a step closer. 'Don't chicken out on me, Sara, or we'll be in real trouble. There's a limit to the number of cast changes an audience will accept. And they at least know *you.*' His eyes glinted mischievously. 'Besides, think how furious Carol will be to know you're playing her part. It's just what that bitch deserves!'

Sara's eyes widened. 'You know what she did, then?'

'Yes—Colin told me. Though I can't figure out why you didn't. Or do you like me to think badly of you?'

'I tried to tell you,' she said indignantly, 'but you were so busy condemning me, you wouldn't listen.'

He nodded, remembering. 'We must be centipedes, you and I.'

'Why?'

'We're always starting off on the wrong foot!'

Sara couldn't help laughing, and he joined in; the first joke they had genuinely shared. Then he grew serious again.

'Will you play Magda?' he urged.

Realising she was cornered, Sara gave in. 'When is Sheena Roberts arriving?' she asked.

'In two weeks.'

'Not before? That means I'll be learning the Magda role during the day and still have to play Daisy at night!'

'I'm afraid so. It'll be tough, but you're a little strong girl!' Benedict half smiled. 'Strange, isn't it? You hate my guts, yet you're saving my show.'

'And sixty other jobs,' she reminded him.

He appreciated the point, as evidenced by the slight inclination of his head. 'Fate plays tricks on all of us, Sara. Who knows, if you see enough of me, you could end up liking me!'

'I don't believe in miracles.'

'Strictly business, eh?'

'Always, where you're concerned.'

'OK, I'll let you have the last word on that,' he grinned. 'Right now, the show's my number one priority.'

'Mine too.'

'Then we agree at last!' He went to the door. 'So you see, miracles do happen!'

And you had the last word after all, Sara thought wryly, and knew he always would.

CHAPTER TEN

FOR Sara the next fourteen days were agony! Not only was she learning the part of Magda during the day and playing Daisy each evening, she also had to fit in sessions for her album. Yet she was reluctant to ask Dick to delay it again, though being the understanding man he was, he offered to do so.

'I don't want you wearing yourself out,' he said, coming to her dressing room one night to collect her. 'As it is, I get an icy glare from your mother every time she sees me.'

'You're imagining it,' Sara expostulated. 'You're too self-conscious where Mother's concerned.'

His shoulders lifted resignedly, and Sara couldn't help feeling sorry for him. It had become his habit to take her out for a late supper two or three times a week—to help her unwind, as he put it. But in reality because he was lonely and did not wish to see any other woman.

She was astonished that a man his age should behave like a lovesick schoolboy, and she could not imagine Benedict acting this way. He would always be in control of himself; never allow a woman to know what he was thinking, what he was feeling.

But maybe when you had such prodigious talent you were incapable of the normal emotions of caring and tenderness. Yet not incapable of passion, she knew, of wanting sexual fulfilment and knowing equally well how to give it. She remembered those few moments with him in the water, and the fiery episode in the gazebo when he had touched a core of desire within her that had left her weak and vulnerable.

With a superhuman effort she concentrated on Dick.

'I don't think Mother's as indifferent to you as she makes out,' she said comfortingly.

'She's certainly not *indifferent*. She can't stand the sight of me!'

Sara couldn't help chuckling, and after a second or two, he joined in.

Dick's company helped lift her gloom, but next day at rehearsals it touched rock bottom again as she stumbled painfully through Magda's lyrics, miserably aware that she couldn't get herself into the character, and that Benedict was listening intently in the front row.

He had been friendlier towards her of late—well, why not, for heaven's sake, when she was saving his show?—and she had caught him watching her with a speculative gleam in his eye, as if trying to decipher her thoughts. Yet even had he done, he wouldn't have understood them, because she didn't understand them herself! Where he was concerned, she was a mass of conflicting opinions: love and hate fighting a battle for supremacy.

Love? Sara was disconcerted that she had associated the word with him. On the other hand, 'like' was far too insipid to describe the emotions he aroused in her.

So lost in thought was she, she was startled to find the object of them beside her, menacingly tall in black slacks and sweater.

'My performance was lousy, wasn't it?' she muttered.

'I can't disagree with you.'

'I don't know how I can improve it.'

'I do. Let's go somewhere quiet and talk.'

Hand light on her arm, he propelled her to her dressing room, his face a shuttered mask she could not decipher. Was he regretting that he'd asked her to play Magda? She wouldn't blame him if he was, nor be surprised if he told her he was looking for someone else to replace her.

He was so close she could smell his aftershave. No, not aftershave—fresh air and newly-cut grass. Strange that someone so sophisticated should remind her of country meadows! But such was his complex character he would always be different from what one expected. Probably a lousy lover, bearing in mind that he looked as if he would be sensational! Yet she knew *that* wasn't true. She could still remember the feel of his hard body and soft hands, the warm sweetness of his tongue.

They reached her dressing room and went inside, and she hurried over to the sink and poured herself a glass of water, anxious to put some distance between them.

'It's pointless you rehearsing with the company, Sara,' Benedict said behind her. 'They'll collapse if they keep working at this pace.'

'So will I!'

'That's why I've decided to coach you myself—at home. It'll be easier and better.'

'It won't be easier until Sheena Roberts gets here and takes over Daisy.'

'Only a week to go,' he consoled. 'She flies in on Sunday, will need a couple of days' rehearsal, and should be ready by Thursday.'

'What a relief that will be.' Sara rubbed her forehead wearily. 'I'm so exhausted I could sleep a week!'

'If you stay in bed on Sunday,' he said bracingly, 'you'll be fine to start work with me on Monday. I'll expect you at ten—my place.'

'Why can't Merrit coach me?' she demanded, panicking at the thought of being alone with him.

'He has his hands full enough. All I want is to go over Magda's character with you. Once you've got a clearer picture of what makes her tick, you should find it much easier to interpret her lyrics.' Benedict's eyes ranged over Sara's face and body. 'You're too thin, you know. What is it? Too much work or too much love?'

'Love?' she echoed sharply.

'Today's *Mail* says you and Dick were "holding hands at Inigo Jones last night and looking deep into each other's eyes".'

'Damn those snoopy journalists,' she said disgustedly. 'They see everything from the bed.'

'That's where associations usually begin!'

'Well, at least you've got the sense not to call them relationships!' she said tartly. 'But as for Dick and me, you're quite wrong. We're just——'

'Good friends? I believe you, darling, though thousands wouldn't!'

Sara frowned. Was that why her mother had been such a cross-patch this morning? Maybe she'd read the *Mail* too and been jealous!

'See you at my place, then,' Benedict repeated, and sauntered away.

For the rest of the week he came to the theatre each evening with a different girl. Yet they were all in the same mould: elegant clothes horses with beautiful faces and vacant expressions. Didn't they bore him, or were they so responsive to him that he didn't care? Yet where was the pleasure in making love to a dummy? But enough about him! She was so obsessed with the man she couldn't think straight. She must put him from her mind.

Easier said than done, Sara thought as she entered his house on Monday and he rose from the piano to greet her, casual in denims, his hair shiny as sealskin as it caught the sunlight.

'Make yourself comfortable and let's begin,' he said in so businesslike a manner that she lost all sense of embarrassment.

For the next few hours he analysed Magda's lines, giving Sara a completely different assessment of the character from the way Carol had interpreted her.

'How come you accepted Carol's version?' she couldn't prevent herself asking as they stopped for coffee and sandwiches.

'Because she couldn't play it any other way. It was a raunchy, funny performance and the audience loved it.'

'Maybe I should give them the same.'

'You aren't the type. Follow your instincts, Sara, and I'll bet they'll love you.'

He swung back to the keyboard, full of restless energy, and she hurriedly swallowed her last mouthful and joined him.

They did not stop again until tea time, which they took on the terrace. When Sara had been here last, the house had been full of people, but now she savoured the tranquil atmosphere and marvelled that such an oasis of quiet could exist in the heart of Kensington.

'Have you lived here long?' she asked.

'It's been the family home for generations, though it was empty for years till I moved in.'

'Why was that?'

'My father was Regular Army and travelled around. He always talked of retiring here, but he was killed in action when I was twelve, and my mother died a year later.'

He fell silent, his expression so sombre that Sara knew he was lost in unhappy memories. She wished she could say something to break his mood but was not sure he would appreciate it, and she was staring down at her hands when he spoke again.

'I used to have the feeling she didn't want to go on living after he died; and, watching her suffer, I vowed I wouldn't let it happen to me.'

'Can one control how deeply one feels?' asked Sara.

'Yes.'

The emphatic answer brooked no argument and Sara,

remembering Barbie, conceded that he had done a pretty good job on himself!

'You're too easy to read,' he mocked. 'You're sitting there hating me!

'Pitying you!' she corrected. 'If you won't accept the lows in life, you'll never sample the highs.'

'I'm satisfied to live in the middle range—except when it comes to music!'

'Ah yes, your music. Well, you can't say your songs aren't full of emotion.'

'The composer isn't necessarily his notes.'

'But the poem is the poet,' she argued, 'and some of your lyrics are pure poetry.'

'What a charming compliment! And coming from you, it's doubly appreciated.'

'I've never denied your talent.'

'Only my integrity!'

Flushing, she jumped up and went inside. She was scared of the intimacy developing between them, and knew it was imperative she keep her distance from him.

'I can't stay much longer,' she called over her shoulder. 'I like to rest for an hour at the theatre before I go on.'

'You can rest here—after you've had a snack.'

'I never eat before a show.'

'That's why you're thin as a rake.'

'*You're* the rake!'

Benedict laughed. 'OK. But don't forget Magda's a full-blooded, voluptuous woman.'

'I can never be voluptuous. I don't have the physique.'

'Voluptuousness is in the mind,' he remarked, resting his gaze on the full curve of her breasts.

Sara felt her nipples stiffen—almost as if he had touched them—and as he lifted his head and their eyes met, colour palpitated in her cheeks. His lower lip moved, almost as if wanting to press the swollen points, and she stepped quickly away from him as he went to the piano.

'Sheena arrived last night,' he said. 'I'll be bringing her to the theatre to see you play Daisy.'

Not waiting for her comment, he went into the opening bars of Magda's first big number. There were three in all, and by the time Sara had run through them, she was limp as a rag.

'Better call it a day,' he pronounced, and as if on cue his manservant wheeled in a trolley holding a little glass bowl brimful of glistening Beluga caviare, while another held wedges of lemon and mounds of chopped egg and finely cut spring onions.

'Good heavens!' gasped Sara.

'Good royalties!' he grinned. 'Eat up.'

She did, ignoring the egg and onion.

'You like caviare plain?' he questioned.

'You can't improve on heaven!'

'It doesn't stop a woman trying!'

'Not that I'm a judge of caviare,' she went on, ignoring his remark. 'I had it for the first time with Dick.'

'How serious is it between you?' asked Bendict. 'I know what you said the other day, but you appear to be seeing a great deal of each other and . . .'

He paused, waiting, but Sara went on eating, reluctant to explain that it was Dick's way of seeing her mother.

'Do I hear wedding bells?' he persisted.

'Not for the moment. But I'll let you know when to start listening.'

'Thanks. All I need are more changes in the cast.'

So the musical was all that concerned him! She should have known.

'Have a snooze while I go change,' he said, pushing back his chair. 'Then I'll run you to the theatre.'

'There's no need—I'll call a cab.'

'I have to go to town anyway to collect Sheena.'

Was he sexually involved with the girl? Sara wondered, then irritably told herself it wasn't her affair with *whom* he had an affair.

Yet as he went out, she mentally followed him upstairs, visualising him shedding his clothes, seeing the ripple of corded muscles, the firmness of strong thighs. What was happening to her! She couldn't remember being so physically aware of a man. With a groan she turned her face into the pillow.

She must have fallen asleep, for the next thing she knew Benedict was shaking her gently awake. Looking up, she once more saw the well-tailored Lothario, his impeccably cut suit drawing attention to his broad shoulders and narrow hips. His hair glistened as though still wet from a shower, and a dark lock fell forward as he bent over her. No wonder he had to fight off the women—and she'd be among them if she didn't watch out!

'You look more rested,' he said softly. 'That little snore did you good.'

'I never snore!'

'You're a great mimic, then!'

Laughing, Sara swung her feet off the settee, but as she went to stand, his hand on her arm prevented her.

'You're trembling, Sara. Are you afraid of me?'

'Don't flatter yourself!'

'I've never needed to before. You're the only girl I know who acts the hedgehog with me.'

'I'm immune to you,' she assured him.

'I don't believe you.'

'That's *your* problem, then.' She tried to pull free of him, but he still held her.

'Tell me you're in love with Dick and I won't bother you again.'

'Leave Dick out of it,' she flared. 'Why can't you accept that I don't give a damn about it?'

'Prove it.'

'How?'

'By kissing me.'

Too late Sara guessed his intention, and before she could escape, his mouth was on hers, his arms wrapped tightly around her waist.

As a kiss, it was the most deliberately provocative; a soft, persistent movement of mouth on mouth, with an occasional delicate flick of tongue brushing her closed lips. All the while his hands roamed her body: gentle on her back and waist, firm as they pressed her buttocks, drawing them against his hard stomach until she felt the tremor shaking him and the involuntary movement of his hips.

With a superhuman effort Sara forced herself to stand motionless, concentrating on everything except the man holding her. At first it was easy, but as his mouth grew more persuasive and his tongue more insistent, she found it impossible to remain quiescent. As he sensed it, his gentleness dissolved, and he roughly prised her lips apart and drained the sweet moisture within, and she breathed in the warmth and sweet taste of him.

Passion flared, would not be denied as she grasped him close. He groaned deep in his throat, and she felt the dampness on his skin, the shaking of his body as he fought for self-control.

But she had no intention of letting him achieve it! He had wanted her surrender, and now she wanted his! After all, why not? Why fight her need of him? Why not let him see she was a woman of passion, as ready for satisfaction as he was?

Aware of her sudden response, Benedict's tongue probed her mouth more deeply, darting erotically in and out, the stabbing movements so like the final act of love that she arched against him feverishly. With a groan he pressed her down upon the settee, and as she sank back on the mound of cushions, he fell upon her, not heavy enough to crush her, but close enough for her to feel the swelling force of his desire.

'Beautiful Sara,' he muttered thickly, his hands finding the zip of her dress and skilfully undoing it.

The bodice fell away and he placed his mouth to the curving fullness of her breast, then swiftly encompassed her stiff nipples, one to suck with his lips, the other to massage with his fingertips. She moaned in ecstasy, and he prised her legs apart and lay between them, the heat of his arousal threatening to burn away her last vestige of control.

With shaking hands Sara pulled open his shirt and dug her fingers in the mat of dark hair on his chest. It was damp with perspiration and she bent her head and pressed her lips to it, her hips moving sinuously beneath his.

Unexpectedly Benedict stilled her roving hands. 'No,' he said thickly. 'Be still, or I won't be responsible for what happens!'

Tenderly he stroked her hair and flushed face, then eased himself off her. Her skirt had ridden up and he traced his fingers over the smooth skin of her thigh, then slid them inside her silken panties to feel the silkier inner warmth that guarded, with protective folds, the very core of her being.

Light as a feather his fingertips caressed the downy mound, but did not penetrate. Flame seared through her body, and wave upon wave of desire sent her arms around his neck to pull him down to her again, her legs entwining his to keep him close.

His hold tightened momentarily, then with a muffled exclamation he pushed her away and stood up.

'Now's not the time,' he said softly. 'And it certainly isn't the place!'

With practised ease he buttoned his shirt and smoothed his hair, and watching him, Sara hated him for the swiftness with which he returned to normality.

Slowly she sat up, zipped up her dress and put on her shoes. Amazingly, her movements were as steady as his, though inside she was shaking. She had never responded to a man this way, and it marked a watershed in her life.

'I won't apologise for what happened,' he said. 'We both enjoyed it too much.'

The word 'enjoyed' sent a frisson of shock through her. How prosaic he made it seem! Yet maybe that was how he saw it—like having a bath or a shave! Tears of mortification burned her eyes and she blinked them away before he saw them.

Turning her back on him, she crossed over to the mirror on the far wall, thankful to find her face didn't reflect her thoughts. But it certainly reflected the passion she had shared with him, for wild roses bloomed in her cheeks and stars seemed trapped in her eyes. She lowered her lids to hide their brilliance, though she could have saved herself the bother, for Benedict was already striding from the room, murmuring that she would be late if she didn't hurry!

Chilled by his attitude, debased if truth be told, Sara followed him to the car.

He drove fast but carefully, seemingly content not to talk, for which she was grateful, for it gave her the chance to think things out.

Why had his lovemaking shattered her so? After all, she was no innocent, overwhelmed by a first kiss. Was it because he was Benedict Peters, the most successful composer of his generation? Many woman were 'turned on' by celebrities, though she had never considered herself to be among them. So was it the man himself? It was the most obvious answer and showed her how easily he could turn her life upside down.

Thank heavens he had no idea of the turmoil he had unleashed. As far as he was concerned her response had been par for the course, no more, no less! And for that she should be grateful.

'If you're free for supper tonight——' he said, breaking the silence.

'I'm not.'

'With Sheena and myself,' he went on, ignoring her interruption.

Mortified at misunderstanding him, Sara said quickly, 'I'm seeing Dick.'

'We'll make it a foursome.'

She shrugged, accepting the inevitable, and did not speak again until they drew up outside the stage door.

'I'm willing to continue rehearsing at your house, Benedict, but I don't want a repetition of this afternoon.'

'Pity. I thought we made wonderful music together.'

'At the piano only.'

'I didn't get that impression.'

'Maybe not. As I said to you before, you're a sexy man and I'm a normal young woman.'

'So how about us having a normal relationship?'

Sara hid her anger. Was jumping into bed with a man just because you fancied him considered the 'norm' these days? Heaven help morality and family life if it was!

'Just because I have an itch,' she said coldly, 'it doesn't mean I should scratch it every time!'

'How about from time to time?'

'At *no* time, thanks. I don't care for casual sex.'

'Tall oaks from little acorns grow,' he said whimsically.

'Not if they fall on barren ground! And my feelings for you are very barren.'

'Ah well, one can't win 'em all.'

'What's one among so many?' she said lightly, and with a cool wave, left him, glad he didn't know how deeply his last remark had cut.

*   *   *

As Sara changed into her costume, she knew with certainty that Benedict would be a perfect lover. Yet how perfect would he be for her if there was no corresponding closeness of spirit? Although he was obviously satisfied by a one-dimensional relationship—if his behaviour was anything to go by—she would quickly find it devoid of meaning. On the other hand, a few weeks with him might get him out of her system.

Or make her fall more deeply under his spell. That was always the danger.

Even now he loomed so large on her horizon she could see no one else, think of no one else. Only Benedict. Appalled at where her thoughts had taken her, she felt the stick of rouge slip from her trembling hand and turned away from the mirror.

Yet the truth had to be faced, and she forced herself to do so. She was in love with him!

A voice outside the door warned her it was fifteen minutes to curtain rise. Barely conscious of what she was doing, she finished her make-up, welcoming the theatrical mask almost as though it would serve to hide her feelings. And hide them she must, for even without the lesson of Barbie, she knew Benedict could destroy her life.

Returning to her dressing room after the finale, she found Dick there. He had spoken to Benedict in the interval and knew they were having supper with him.

'I said we'd meet him at Scott's,' he told her.

'Fine.' Anxious to hide her face, Sara rummaged along the dress rail, trying to decide between a flowered chiffon and a black silk trouser suit.

The trouser suit won the day, as it did Dick's approval when she emerged from her private bathroom wearing it. It emphasised her slenderness, the material hugging the curve of her hip, the gold piped bodice clinging lovingly to breasts that looked even fuller since she had lost weight.

'You shouldn't be going out with a middle-aged man like me,' he chided as they drove towards Mayfair. 'You should have a proper boy-friend—or better still, an improper one!'

'That's one thing I can do without,' she said soberly. 'Right now I'm concentrating on my career.'

And nothing *but* my career, she reminded herself as they walked across the restaurant to where Benedict sat at a secluded table by the wall.

He rose to greet them and she saw him with new eyes, aware not only of his physical magnetism but his vibrant personality. Instictively she knew he would always be in control of himself and every situation; that nothing would take him by surprise, and that no matter how difficult the odds, he would always come through a winner. It was this belief in himself that gave him his strength.

So engulfed was she by his presence that for an instant she did not see the girl with him. But when she did, she was astounded. Sheena Roberts was—at first glance—an identikit of herself!

A second glance showed this to be only partially true, for the girl's hair was more yellow than amber—and not natural—and her eyes brown and set slightly too close together.

'Your performance was terrific,' Sheena gushed huskily. 'But different from the way *I* intend playing it.'

'Really!' Sara's tone would have frozen salt water, and the gleam in Benedict's eyes showed his awareness of it. Drat him! He was too damned observant. 'How *do* you intend playing it?' she questioned.

'For laughs. At the moment Magda's getting them all.' Sheena clapped her hand to her mouth, as if realising she was talking to the very girl who'd soon be playing the leading part. 'Heck! now I've put my foot in it!'

'Not by accident, I'm sure,' said Sara smooth as glass, and

picked up the menu.

Sheena's mouth tightened, and she slid closer along the seat towards Benedict, her scarlet-tipped fingers caressing his arm.

'I can see Sara and I will get on famously, darling. You never told me what a great sense of humour she has.'

'I wanted you to find out for yourself!'

As supper progressed, Sheena concentrated entirely on him, and only as they reached the coffee stage did she point across the room.

'Isn't that Hoyram Rogers and his wife?'

Benedict nodded, and the girl jumped up. 'Let's go say hello to them. I haven't seen Hyram since we toured together in *The Magician*.'

Benedict allowed himself to be led away, and only then did Sara relax, though she wasn't aware of giving a heartfelt sigh until she heard Dick say, 'Like that, eh? I can see you hate her guts.'

'Am I so obvious?'

'Yes! But you've every right to be. She had her knife out the minute you walked in. She's a typical little go-getter, out to get our composer.'

'Do you think she will?' Sara's heart thumped heavily, though her voice was calm. 'Look at all the others who've tried and failed, and Sheena isn't so extraordinary.'

'Perhaps not. But she's a wily young lady who knows how to get around a man.'

'Sounds as if you're talking from experience!'

'Not mine, my dear. But I've a nephew in LA who got entangled with her. Luckily he soon discovered the only thing she cares about is her career—hence her rushing over, all willing and able!'

'I'd still be surprised if she was able enough to hook Benedict permanently! He's too used to star-struck girls to be taken in by this one.'

'Sheena has something the others haven't.'

'I don't think I want to know what it is!'

'I was going to say talent! You may not like her, but wait till you see her on stage! And she's no fool either, which is something else that would appeal to him. I hear they're pretty close when he's in the States.'

'Must we talk about Benedict's love life?' Sara pretended to yawn.

'I'd talk about mine if I had one,' said Dick somewhat bitterly. 'If I—well, I'll be darned! Look who's over there in the corner.'

Turning, Sara saw Colin and Ella side by side in an alcove, so close together that not even a menu could have come between them!

'Seems we'll soon be hearing wedding bells,' she remarked. 'Colin's the old-fashioned type.'

'Aren't you?'

'I guess I am. But I know how hard it is to mix marriage and children with a demanding career.'

'Not necessarily. It depends if you have an understanding partner. And it would be a big help if he were in a related profession . . .'

Meeting Dick's shrewd brown eyes, Sara was scared he had guessed her feelings. But she had no intention of confirming them. It was her secret, and no one—not even her mother—would ever know.

'I still prefer to concentrate on my career and not get sidetracked,' she said firmly.

'I agree entirely,' commented Benedict, overhearing the last part of the conversation as he and Sheena rejoined them.

'It's a good thing I don't take you seriously,' the American girl trilled. 'Otherwise I'd give up my career this instant and concentrate on *you!*'

'It would get you nowhere, sweetheart. Stay-at-home

women bore me stiff.'

'I'd work out a happy medium if you said the word!'

'Which is why I'm staying dumb!'

Sheena gave a tinkling laugh and rubbed herself against him like a kitten.

Watching the tableau, Sara would have given a great deal to know how seriously Benedict took Sheena's remark, and if he meant his own. Did they have an understanding, or was the girl alone doing the pushing?

As if divining her thoughts, he gave Sara a mocking wink which she met with a cold stare. He obviously enjoyed establishing some form of intimacy with every woman he knew, and she had no intention of falling in with his plans. If only she and Dick could decently leave!

'You look tired, Sara,' Benedict said unexpectedly. 'But you're in the home stretch now. From next week you'll only have your album and Magda to worry about.'

'What a life of idleness,' she murmured. 'How will I fill my time!'

'You sound as if you don't like the theatre,' Sheena said waspishly.

'Let's say I don't find musicals mind-stretching.'

'But Benedict's are sensational.'

'You won't convince Sara of that,' he said, 'and I'm inclined to agree with her.' A tanned hand toyed with a wine glass. 'Which is why I'm considering a musical version of *The Tempest*.'

There was a sudden hush, broken first by Dick.

'You could be on to another winner there.'

'I agree,' Sheena said quickly. 'It's my favourite of all Shakespeare's plays. And I adore Miranda. I hope you'll give me first refusal, darling?'

'I don't think you're quite the type. Actually I've Sara in mind for it.'

Seeing Sheena blanch, Sara was momentarily sorry for

the girl. There'd been no need for Benedict to be quite such a swine!

Yet to her dismay she found she had misjudged him, for as they left the restaurant and he was momentarily alone with her—Sheena and Dick pausing to speak to someone they knew—he said, 'I slapped Sheena down because she was insufferably rude to you. She told me she wanted to talk to you about Daisy, and then she——'

'I don't need you to defend me,' Sara cut in.

'That's what friends are for.'

'You couldn't be friends with a woman. You only see them as conquests.'

'If you're thinking about this afternoon, I apologise. I give you my word it won't happen again.'

'Your word? The way you once gave it to Barbie?'

'Can't you forget her?' he bit out. 'I'm beginning to see the virtue of amnesia!'

Furiously Sara flounced ahead of him, waiting by the exit for Dick to join her.

They left Sheena and Benedict heading towards the Connaught, and Sara ached to know if he was going up to her suite. Oh, God, she thought wearily, is this how I'll be the rest of my life? Longing for him? Jealously wondering how he's spending his nights? Common sense told her to forget him, yet she knew it was impossible as long as she remained in the show.

She was sliding into the front seat of Dick's car when Colin and Ella emerged from the restaurant.

'Hello there!' Colin dashed over. 'I never saw you inside.'

'I don't think you saw anyone except Ella,' she teased.

'We were celebrating,' he admitted. 'I'd like you two to be the first to know we're getting married.'

Sara jumped from the car and hugged him, then kissed Ella. 'I'm so happy for you. When's the happy day?'

'Six weeks Saturday. Then after our honeymoon, I'll be returning to the show. Isn't life wonderful, Sara?'

'It certainly seems to be,' Sara agreed, wishing it were true for herself, and keeping a smile fixed on her face as she watched them go to their car.

'Any regrets?' asked Dick bluntly as they too drove off.

'Not a single one. It's marvellous to get Colin out of my hair. I used to feel so guilty that he was wasting his life hankering after me.'

'Make sure *you* don't do any hankering.'

'That's not likely. I'm a career girl, remember?'

Dick slowed the car to look at her. The overhead street lighting showed his serious expression, and she tried to hide her own.

'I never press confidences, Sara, but I don't think you're as immune to Benedict as you make out.'

Sara had to smile. This was not pressing confidences?

Appreciating why she was amused, Dick looked wry. 'OK, so I'm being pushy! But as I said the first time I took you to dinner, you're young enough to be my daughter. And now, because of my feelings for your mother, I feel as if you almost are. Which is why I want to see you happy.'

'My best way is to keep clear of Benedict.'

'Because of what happened between him and your friend? There are two sides to every situation, you know, and it's unwise to set yourself up as judge and jury. From what I know of him, he's pretty honourable.'

'In business, maybe. In his love life, he's a rat.'

'If you say so.' Dick drew up outside her apartment block. 'I'll be in Australia the next few weeks, but I'll do my best to get back in time for Colin's wedding.'

'See you at the altar, then,' she teased, happy to change the conversation.

'If only that were true,' he sighed, and kissed her goodnight.

Going up in the lift, Sara wished she could find a way of bringing him and her mother together. But she was fast coming to the unhappy conclusion that her mother would never put anyone in her husband's place.

Knowing her own feelings for Benedict, Sara could appreciate why. Her love was still new, yet she could not imagine giving herself to anyone else. So how much harder must it be to contemplate life with another man after twenty years of happy marriage!

On this sober thought she went to bed, but unfortunately not to sleep. For endless hours she lay awake, prey to images of Benedict's body entwined with Sheena's, his hands searching out the same intimacies he had searched out in her own.

Moaning as though in pain, she stumbled into the kitchen to make herself a hot drink, then went into the living room to watch the night sky slowly give way to dawn and another day.

But not to another love, she acknowledged miserably, accepting the fact that she would have to face many more anguished and lonely nights.

CHAPTER ELEVEN

SHEENA took over from Sara the following Thursday, and Sara—who was not stepping into the Magda role till after the weekend—found herself with four days free.

It was like being let out of prison! She toyed with the idea of going to Paris; even of taking her mother on Concorde for a whirlwind tour of New York. But she foolishly mentioned both options to Tony, who shot them down by insisting she spend the time putting the finishing touches to her album.

Knowing he was right, she gave in, and that evening decided to go to the theatre—a busman's holiday, but a necessary one—to watch Sheena's performance.

The girl hadn't been lying when she'd said she intended playing Daisy for laughs, and Sara's anger rose higher with every guffaw from the audience. If she allowed Sheena to get away with this interpretation, *she'd* have to play Magda for laughs—as Carol had—which she knew wouldn't please Benedict.

First thing next morning she called Merrit and told him of her misgivings.

'I couldn't agree with you more,' he said. 'But Sheena's Benedict's choice and I refuse to get into a hassle with her.'

'But you're the director!'

'Look, my dear, she's a big name and she's helping us out of a hole. It's only till Ella gets back, so it's something I can live with.'

'Well, I can't,' said Sara angrily.

'Then have it out with Benedict.'

'I damn well will!'

Crossly she telephoned him. He was out, his manservant

142

said, but was expected back in an hour, and though she loathed the prospect of seeing him, she decided to go to his house and let him know exactly how she felt.

She arrived there ahead of him. Thomas showed her into the living room, and she wandered around it, savouring the lovely objets d'art and paintings.

Not for Benedict the obvious French impressionists, or Fabergé or jade, but intricate Winslow Homer water-colours, and shelves of wondrously glazed Chinese glass vases of the Ch'ien Lung period. One piece particularly delighted her, and she leaned forward for a closer look. It was the most skilled treatment of glass she had seen: brown carving on a golden background, made to resemble tortoiseshell.

'Pick it up and touch it if you like,' a deep voice said, and she swung round to see the man who was never far from her thoughts.

They had not met since their dinner at Scott's, and she was quick to notice lines around his eyes that had not been there then. No doubt the result of burning the candle at both ends, she thought sourly.

'Pick it up,' he urged. 'It has a lovely tactile quality.'

'I'd be scared in case I dropped it.'

'It's insured.'

'But irreplaceable, I should imagine.'

'Inanimate objects have a man-made value,' he shrugged. 'Only life is irreplaceable.

'I still feel happier leaving it on the shelf!' She did not meet his eyes. 'Sorry to barge in on you like this, but I phoned earlier and Thomas said you had no other appointments.'

'Don't apologise for coming to see me.' He sank down into an armchair and waved her to do the same.

She chose one some distance away, careful to avoid the settee, though the mere sight of it set her pulses racing.

'So why are you here, Sara?' He put his hands behind his

head, a gesture that drew attention to the flatness of his stomach. 'Is it because of Sheena's Daisy, your Magda, or good old Barbie?'

'I've no intention of discussing Barbie,' Sara said witheringly.

'Does that mean we've wiped the slate clean and can start again?'

If only we could, she thought, resisting the mad urge to fling herself into his arms and say she'd forget his past as long as she could be the only one in his future. Some hope she had! Regardless of what Dick said, there would always be a Sheena in Benedict's life. He might be attracted to herself, but it wouldn't keep him permanently out of another woman's bed.

'From the look on your face,' he murmured, breaking into her thoughts, 'the slate's still full. But not to worry. As fleas are to a dog, so your dislike is to me! Fact is, I enjoy your antagonism. It keeps me on my toes.' He lowered his arms and leaned forward. 'Now tell me why you're here.'

'Because Sheena's turning Daisy into a clown—which alters my role—and is also spoiling her song in the second act.'

'Ruining it,' he stated. 'Not spoiling.'

Sara gaped at him, and his mouth tilted sardonically.

'Did you think Sheena's attractions blinded me to her faults?' he queried.

'They would most men.'

'I'm not most.'

Strolling over to the piano, he ran his hands across the keyboard. A homing pigeon returning to base, Sara thought, and guessed that in moments of stress or joy, this was where he would turn.

'A man of my rakish reputation,' he went on, 'is never blind to a woman's flaws. I'm surprised you didn't realise that.'

'I thought you regarded Sheena differently.'

'Are you fishing?' Even from across the room the mocking glitter in his eyes was unmistakable.

'Can one fish in shark-infested waters?'

'Who's the shark, angel face? Me or Sheena?'

'Both, I should think!'

He laughed. 'You're getting sharper by the minute. Soon you won't only be drawing blood, you'll be sucking it!'

Anger vied with amusement and lost the day as Sara joined in his laughter. When they finally stopped, the tension was gone between them, and she could almost believe they really were the friends he had not so long ago asked her to be. And she could easily have been friends with him had she not loved him. Watching his fingers feather the keyboard, light as if he were touching a woman's body— her body—she quickly averted her gaze.

'I'm taking the second act number away from Sheena,' Benedict announced unexpectedly. 'She'll never sing it as well as you.'

'Pity. It's a show-stopper.'

'If I change the lyrics, we can make it Magda's.'

'Sheena will kill me!' laughed Sara.

'Cats have nine lives, kitten!'

'You think it was catty of me to come here?'

'No—it was intelligent. If you ever have doubts about the show, you're entitled to air them.'

He started singing Sheena's number with new words, and Sara marvelled at his ability to change the lyrics as he went along, realising for the first time how wrong it was to judge him by normal standards. People driven by great talent required special understanding. Had she appreciated this from the beginning, things might have been different between them.

Yet they could still never have been lovers. Allowing Benedict to come too close would have destroyed her.

With a start she realised he had finished playing, and she hurriedly nodded approval.

'It's a superb switch around, but I won't do it. I wasn't joking about Sheena being furious. She'd really make my life difficult, and it's not worth it.'

'I've written something else for her,' came the laconic reply.

'That's exactly how you placated Carol!'

'I know. Like I said, all women are sisters under the skin.'

'How cynical you are! One day your lady friends will tumble to you.'

'They tumble already—straight into my bed!'

'You're modest too!'

'Factual, angel face. Sorry if it offends your moral rectitude.'

'You're not sorry in the least. You enjoy overturning barriers.'

'Only false ones. You're no more moral than Sheena. A little more persuasion on my part the other day, and you'd have ended up in my bed too!'

Sara jumped to her feet, furious. 'Don't kid yourself! Necking on the couch is a long way from—from——'

'Want me to prove it isn't?'

Stealthy as a cat he advanced on her, and she backed away. 'Stop playing games, Benedict. I'm not one of your women!'

For a long moment he regarded her, drawn eyebrows darkening his eyes, his body tense as a spring.

'You'd like me to make a fool of myself by falling in love, wouldn't you?' he asked softly.

'How right you are. What a laugh to finally see the biter bit!'

'Still judging me, eh?'

'You could try defending yourself,' she said pointedly.

'I've nothing to defend.' As though tiring of the interplay, he returned to the piano. 'While you're here, we might as well run through Magda again. I'm free for the rest of the day.'

The last thing Sara wanted was to spend it with him, but she could not refuse his offer.

'It's for the good of the show,' he added pointedly, and reddening, she slipped off the jacket of her linen suit and joined him at the keyboard.

As before, they worked regardless of time, stopping only when Thomas told them lunch was waiting for them on the terrace. Benedict drank no alcohol, though he offered Sara wine, which she declined. Instead they both sipped peach juice, which went well with the scallop and cucumber mousse that was followed by raspberries and cream.

'You eat like a child,' Benedict commented amusedly, and only then did she realise she was licking her spoon.

Hastily, she put it down. She had always loved sweet things, and was disconcerted that she had been so relaxed with Benedict that she had forgotten herself.

'Care for some more?' he teased.

She shook her head, though not without regret. 'I daren't—or I'll end up a barrel at forty.'

'You'll probably have a dull and doting husband by then, so I'm sure it won't matter.'

How easily he saw her sharing her life with someone else! A bitter sweet vision of what might have been made her voice sharp.

'I can appreciate the "doting", but why make my husband dull?'

'Because you're searching for a paragon—not a real man. And paragons are always dull!'

Nervous of continuing the conversation, Sara rose. Simultaneously Benedict did the same, the action bringing them so close that she felt his breath fan her hair.

'We're obviously meant to have the next dance,' he said whimsically, and before she could step back, drew her into his arms and kissed her.

Instinctively she responded, her lips parting to him. I love you, she cried silently. Oh, Benedict, how I love you!

His kiss deepened and his hands pressed her body closer to his. His heart was pounding and the stiffening between his loins showed the swift rise of his desire. But Sara knew it was a desire he would feel for any attractive woman, and she despised herself for surrendering to him. Yet she longed to savour this glorious moment, knowing it might be the only one she would have with him. Limb against limb, tongue against tongue, they remained close, hands searching, bodies trembling as passion rose high.

'I want you,' he muttered thickly. 'God, I want you!'

Sara echoed the words voicelessly, every instinct urging her to give herself to him. But she could never be his momentary partner in passion; a plaything to be discarded when his ardour cooled. Unless his need of her was accompanied by love, she would be left more achingly empty than before.

'Sara, *please*,' he said huskily. 'Let me love you.'

Hearing him mouth a word she knew was meaningless to him, she pushed him violently away.

'It wouldn't be love, Benedict. It would be lust!'

Unsteadily she straightened her dress, furious to see he was completely composed except for a slightly heightened colour, and the errant lock of dark hair that persistently fell upon his forehead.

'I won't apologise this time either,' he said abruptly.

'I didn't expect you to. The one thing you're not is a liar!'

'And the one thing *you* are is consistent.'

His tone was bored, as if he found her dislike a tedium he no longer cared to cope with. But even as he turned to go inside, a slight, brown-haired young man stepped out through the French windows.

'Chris!' Benedict stopped in his tracks. 'I wasn't expecting you.' His tone was so curt, the young man flushed.

'Sorry, Ben. I thought you'd be free. Yesterday you said——'

'That was yesterday. Now I'm rehearsing.'

'I see.'

Chris's tone was dry, the glance he gave Sara so telling, it was her turn to colour.

'You don't see at all,' Benedict said irritably. 'This is Sara James—our new Magda—and we're going over the role. By the piano, I hasten to add, not on the couch!'

Embarrassed, the young man came closer. As he did, Sara saw he was older than she had first thought: late twenties rather than late teens, and good-looking in a boyish way, with freckled features, warm brown eyes and unruly hair of the same colour.

'Since Ben seems reluctant to introduce us,' he said with a friendly grin, 'I'll do it myself. I'm his cousin.'

His cousin! If he was also a doctor, then Barbie must have been his patient! Curiosity would not be held in check, but she let it loose guilelessly.

'Are you a composer too?' she asked.

'Only of medical prescriptions!'

'I see.' She pretended to hesitate, and was careful to avoid Benedict's eyes. 'I believe you were Barbie's doctor.'

'Right. But she left me when she—er—when——'

'When I left *her*,' Benedict finished for him. 'Now did you come over for any particular reason, Chris, or merely to kill an hour?'

'What a way to describe a social call!' The younger man seemed oblivious of the sarcasm. 'It's my free afternoon and I popped in to say hello.' He moved closer to the table. 'Hmm, scallop mousse—my favourite! Mind if I help myself to what's left?'

'You will, anyway,' his cousin said sardonically. 'Would you like some fresh coffee too?'

'I thought you'd never offer!' Chris sat down and proceeded to demolish the remainder of the mousse. 'I've been up since five delivering a baby—I wish women wouldn't insist on having them at home—and I'm famished.'

'Since five?' echoed Sara, watching with amusement as the mousse disappeared, and what was left of the raspberries and cream quickly followed suit. 'Was it a difficult birth, then?'

'Not really. But I went straight on to my surgery and have only just got through. I must say I feel a whole lot better now I have some food inside me. And I *would* like that coffee!'

Muttering beneath his breath, Benedict stomped round the side of the terrace to the kitchen, giving Sara the distinct impression that he was reluctant to leave them alone.

'How well do you know Barbie?' Chris asked casually.

'She's my best friend. We grew up together.' Sara hesitated. 'How long were you her doctor?'

'About a year. As Ben said, she found it embarrassing to stay with me after they stopped seeing each other.'

'Pity.' Sara liked the look of Chris, for he had a sympathetic air. 'You know, for a long while she was terrified of being left with a limp.'

'I told her she wouldn't.'

'You saw her afterwards then?'

Chris looked discomfited. He glanced towards the end of the terrace as though afraid his cousin might overhear, and when he answered, his voice was quick and low.

'I spoke to her on the phone, actually, when she came out of hospital. I checked on their medical report and thought I should reassure her that she'd recover completely.'

Benedict came towards them with a cup of coffee, and set it on the table. 'Drink up and go,' he advised.

'Thanks, cousin.' Cheerily Chris did so in one gulp. 'Is that why you made it half cold?'

'You catch on quick, mate! But come to dinner tomorrow if you're free.'

'Will do.'

With a grin, Chris left, and Benedict returned to the piano.

'Come on, Sara, we've work to do.'

And work they did, going over and over the song he had rewritten for her, to make sure the lyrics fitted Magda's character.

'You know, you've made her a much warmer woman,' he said an hour later, as he flexed his fingers to rest them for a moment. 'But that's because you're a first-rate actress.'

Sara flushed at the compliment, and he smiled.

'We may fight in our personal lives, angel face, but professionally I can't fault you. Now let's take the last verse from the top.'

As Sara went to do so, she heard a throaty voice in the hall. Sheena! Oh lord! the last person she wanted to see. Why hadn't Benedict warned her she was coming?

Before he could rise from the piano, the girl swept in, blonde tresses in careful disarray, high heels clicking on the parquet floor.

'Sorry to be early, Benedict, but——' Her smile froze as she saw Sara, but quickly regaining control, she glided forward. 'I didn't realise you weren't alone, darling. Hope I'm not interrupting anything?'

'You mean you hope you are!' he chuckled.

'How well you know me!' She leaned against him for an instant before settling into an armchair.

In a clinging orange dress, and with her yellow eyes and hair, she reminded Sara of a marmalade cat. No, a tiger, she amended, seeing the eyes narrow at her, and the scarlet-tipped fingers curl against the suede seat, almost as if yearning to rake them down Sara's face.

'Help yourself to a drink while I go change,' said Benedict.

'Are we eating here or out?' Sheena enquired.

'Here, I think, if that's all right with you?'

'It's what I hoped you'd say. Then I can have you to myself.'

Her melting look hardened as it encompassed Sara, who immediately picked up her bag.

'Hang on a moment, Sara,' said Benedict. 'I'd like to give you a copy of the new lyrics.'

As he walked out to get them, Sheena raised an eyebrow. 'What new lyrics?'

'For one of my songs.'

Knowing Benedict as she did, Sara was convinced he had deliberately left the ball in her court. But she was darned if she'd play it for him! Let *him* be the one to tell Sheena he had taken away her show-stopping number! However, she had reckoned without the girl's persistence.

'What song? Don't stand there innocent as a nun! Tell me.'

Reluctantly Sara did, astounded when Sheena nonchalantly shrugged and settled further back in her chair, curling her legs beneath her.

'I suppose you went all dewy-eyed on him and asked him to give it to you,' she stated matter-of-factly.

'I most certainly didn't.'

'You mean he offered all by himself? Pull the other one, honey! You knew it was a show-stopper and you wanted it for yourself. Well, have it with my compliments.'

Sara's amazement grew, and Sheena's lips curled in a sly smile.

'You expected me to be furious, didn't you? Which shows what a lousy judge of character you are. Benedict's too important to me for me to be angry with him over a song. Now if you'd tried taking *him* from me, it would be a different story. He's a property I've no intention of relinquishing.'

'A property? Is that how you see him?'

'Property, possession, lover—take your pick. But Benedict's mine, so save yourself the aggro of trying to take him away from me.'

With an effort for which she awarded herself top marks, Sara flung back her head and laughed.

'Poor Sheena, how blind can you be? Benedict may be many things, but no one woman can ever call him hers!'

'Because he plays around? That's meaningless. It's who he comes home to at night that counts.'

'You really don't care if he's unfaithful?'

'Sure I care,' said Sheena. 'But if it's a question of having him on his own terms or not at all, then I'm prepared to take what I can get. That's why I've lasted so long with him. He's been a lone wolf for years, and I'd be a fool to pull the rope too tight. Once we're married—have a kid, maybe— things will change.' Sheena's voice softened, though it seemed more with anticipation of controlling Benedict than with maternal love. 'He's crazy about kids, you know, and one of his own will do more to clip his wings than anything I can dream up between the sheets!'

Sickened by what she was hearing, Sara longed to run away and never see Sheena's triumphant face again. But misery held her paralysed, and all she could do was stand and listen.

'As soon as we open on Broadway, we're getting married,' Sheena went on. 'But keep it under your hat. Benedict hates personal publicity, so we haven't told a soul.'

Sara felt as though she were being pulled apart limb from limb, though her voice didn't give her away.

'I think the two of you should be very happy together. You obviously both have the same attitude to life.'

The yellow head nodded complacently. 'When you're marrying a genius you have to take the good with the bad. Or should I say the bed!'

There was nothing Sara dared say to this, and silently she went into the hall. She couldn't possibly wait for Benedict's lyrics. Her hand was on the door knob when she heard his step behind her, and turning blindly she grasped the sheet of paper from him and stuffed it into her bag.

'I'm sorry Sheena arrived when she did,' he said quietly. 'I'd forgotten she was coming.'

'I'd have had to leave soon anyway.' Sara marvelled that she could appear so normal. 'I'm going out to dinner.'

'I'd planned on having a serious talk with you,' he went on as if he had not heard her. 'I've several things to say.'

'Nothing I want to hear.'

'How do you know till you've heard me?'

'Because I'm totally uninterested in you, I know you're incapable of loyalty to a woman, Benedict, but don't you at least have any self-respect?'

Anger flared in his face as he stepped forward. Afraid he was going to hit her, Sara jumped back, feeling a fool as she realised he was only going to open the door for her.

'It's definitely time you left,' he ground out. 'There's nothing more tedious than a woman who repeats herself!'

Pushing past him, she ran down the path, so blinded by tears she stumbled and nearly fell. Luckily Benedict wasn't there to see, for he had closed the door on her, as if he could not wait to get her out of his sight.

Returning home, Sara finally acknowledged that she couldn't remain in the show. She'd call John tonight and leave him to make the arrangements. Only the other day he'd mentioned something about the producers offering her a longer contract at double her present fee, but all the money in the world couldn't persuade her to stay in Benedict's.

A quick, clean break was her only salvation.

CHAPTER TWELVE

THOUGH Sara got on well with her mother, she realised the disadvantages of their living together when she returned home.

'You look as if you've lost a pound and found a penny,' came the penetrating comment. 'Another eruption with Benedict?'

'Our relationship's an ongoing volcano,' Sara sighed.

'What caused the explosion today?'

'I'd rather not talk about it. If you haven't prepared supper, what say we go to Gavvers?'

'Lovely idea. I haven't eaten out for ages.'

'More fool you. Dick's always asking you.'

'I know. But he's *your* friend, not mine.'

Knowing her mother's obstinacy, Sara let the matter drop. Dick was a fool not to let her mother know how he felt about her. She couldn't see Benedict letting things go on unresolved.

Always Benedict! The thought of him was so nerve-racking, she picked up the receiver and dialled John. She had never called him at his home before, but he was her agent, so what the hell!

'You ill?' he asked anxiously, when he heard her voice.

'No, I'm fine. But I want to leave the show. John, are you there? Did you hear me?'

'Sure I heard you. And I wish I hadn't! In fact I'm going to close my eyes and count to ten, and hope that when I open them again I'll find I've been dreaming!'

'It's no dream,' she assured him. 'I want out.'

'Out of your head, you mean! You're taking over the lead role on Monday. You can't walk out!'

'I've no contract, and if I give a month's notice——'

'Your name will be mud! It could hurt your career badly, Sara.'

'I don't care,' she said obstinately.

'You're suffering from nerves,' he said gently. 'I know exactly what you're going through, and I beg you not to do anything hastily. Play Magda in front of an audience before you make a final decision. When you see how much they love you, you'll change your mind.'

'I won't. I'm serious, John.'

There was a short silence.

'OK,' he said heavily. 'You're the client. But you owe it to the cast to wait till Merrit can find a big name to replace you.'

Appreciating the sense of this, Sara gave in. 'Just make sure they find a replacement soon. If there's any stalling, I'll quit.'

'I never thought I'd see the day when *you* got temperamental,' were John's final words as he put down the telephone.

Me neither, she admitted silently, and wished she could turn back the clock and find herself in a provincial opera company again!

But on Monday night she was far from the provinces as she stepped on stage as Magda. For the first few seconds her limbs seemed made of cotton wool and her voice was a thin quaver, then her professionalism won the day and she began to feel herself into the character, all the subtle changes Benedict had suggested falling miraculously into place.

As the curtain fell on the finale, the audience gave her a standing ovation, showing Sara exactly what John meant about the wonder of applause. Yet her need to put space between herself and Benedict remained dominant, for it was the only way she could forget him.

Staggering beneath the weight of bouquets, she returned

to her dressing room. It was crowded with well-wishers; only Benedict was absent, and she was both glad and furious.

'We're throwing a party for you at the Savoy,' Merrit declared. 'You were bloody marvellous!'

'I couldn't face any more people tonight.'

Interpreting the flatness in her voice as another manifestation of nerves, Merrit signalled everyone to leave.

'You're only tired from the strain of everything,' he told her the instant they were alone. 'But a week from now and you'll be romping through the part.' He patted his breast pocket. 'Which reminds me, I've got a contract for you to sign. John's negotiated a fabulous deal for you.'

'I'm not signing. I've already told him.'

'What do you mean you're not signing?'

'I'm going to leave.'

'We'll talk about it tomorrow,' he said quickly.

'My answer will be the same, Merrit. There are personal reasons,' she added to forestall his protests, 'and I won't change my mind.'

'Perhaps I can change it for you,' a deep voice said, and with a shock Sara saw Benedict on the threshold. 'Leave us, Merrit,' he ordered.

The director walked out, and Sara sent up a silent prayer of thanks that she was still wearing her stage make-up; at least she could hide behind its mask.

'I'm going to the States in a few weeks,' Benedict told her quietly. 'We're opening on Broadway mid-October and I'll be there till spring. So you see there won't be any problem about you avoiding me. I assume that's why you're talking about quitting?'

'Yes.'

'Well, now it's unnecessary. You've worked hard for success, Sara. It would be a shame to let a man like me stop you getting to the top!'

'I can't believe you're interested in safeguarding my

career,' she said scathingly.

'I'm interested in safeguarding my musical,' he corrected, and turned to the door, his profile hard to read. 'To satisfy my curiosity, though, is Barbie still the only reason for your antagonism?'

'You've asked me that before,' she said evenly, and began unpinning the false curls from the top of her head. 'Naturally it prejudiced me, but once I got to know you for myself it merely endorsed my opinion. You're the tops as a composer, but the bottoms as a human being.'

'On which happy note we'll say goodbye!'

The door closed behind him, and Sara buried her head in her hands and burst into tears.

True to his word Benedict kept out of her way for the rest of the month. Yet some sixth sense made her tinglingly aware of his presence whenever he came to the theatre, even though she rarely caught sight of him.

As Merrit had predicted, she soon took the new role in her stride. But she missed Dick and counted the days till his return from Australia. She even missed Colin—something she hadn't expected—which only proved what a low emotional state she was in.

However, her spirits lifted when Ella asked her to be maid of honour at her wedding.

'I've no sisters,' she explained, 'and even if I had, I'd still ask you. After all, if you hadn't pushed Colin my way . . .'

'He'd still have discovered he loved you,' Sara finished. 'Though it might have taken him a while longer. And I'll be delighted to be maid of honour as long as I don't have to wear pink!'

'White, actually. I've always dreamed of an all white wedding.'

Choosing the dress was fun, though not unnaturally Sara suffered a pang or two. Had she not fallen for Benedict it might have been *her* bridal gown she was choosing, *her* maid of honour she was accompanying.

'Why the long face?' her mother asked the night before the wedding.

'I wasn't aware I had one.'

'You hardly have anything else when we're alone. I suppose you're missing Dick?'

'Very much. I can't wait for him to get back.'

As if on cue, the telephone rang, and she picked it up and heard his voice.

'Dick! We were just talking about you. Are you here or in Australia?'

'Here, of course. I told you I'd try to get back for the wedding. How are you and your mother getting to the church?'

'In a white Rolls, no less! I'm maid of honour.'

'That's great.' He paused, then added quietly: 'Is your mother well?'

'Fine!'

'Do you think she missed me?'

'I'm glad you had a successful trip,' Sara enthused.

'So she's in the room! If I didn't have a business meeting scheduled, I'd come round and see you both.'

'You should be going to bed, not to a meeting,' Sara reproved. 'You must be jet-lagged.'

'I like it when you worry over me,' he chuckled, then gave a faint sigh. 'Give your mother my love if you think she'll accept it.'

'I'll do that.' Replacing the receiver, Sara turned to see her mother absorbed in the latest *Vogue*. 'Dick sends you his love,' she said.

'What? Who?' Helen James looked up.

'Dick sends you his love. He's just back from Australia.'

'Stupid man!' her mother muttered. 'He's crazy to go to a meeting when he's just flown half-way round the world.'

Sara's eyes widened. So her mother hadn't been as intent on her magazine as she'd pretended! But it was best to play dumb and let her darling parent think she was pulling the wool over her daughter's eyes!

'I'm for an early night,' she murmured, rising. 'See you in the morning.'

It couldn't have been a more glorious one, mellow with the golden glow of a lovely October. In white organza, with full skirt floating around her like a cloud, and tight bodice clinging to her slender waist, Sara looked a bride herself.

'You're so beautiful,' her mother said huskily as she came into the hall and saw her.

'You look pretty good too. More like the *sister* of the maid of honour.'

Indeed, her mother had never looked better in a hyacinth-blue wool suit, a jaunty Breton beret giving her an unusual sauciness.

'I wish *you* had a special man,' Sara said impulsively. 'Dad wouldn't have wanted you to remain alone.'

'I'm perfectly happy as I am,' her mother said coldly, and marched down to the car.

The church was packed; not only with family, friends and cast, but with the media and the crowds who always came to gawp at celebrities. Ella and Colin glowed with joy in each other, and Sara's eyes misted with tears as she watched them at the altar.

If only it were me and Benedict, she thought miserably as she bent to arrange the bride's train, and wondered if she would ever meet anyone who would make her forget him. She doubted it. Whoever she married—if she ever did—he could never be more than second best.

'Dearly beloved,' the minister intoned, and the service began. Soon it was time for her to step forward and take Ella's bouquet, and as Sara turned to move back to her place, her eyes lifted from the fragile petals and met those of the lean-bodied, black-haired man in an aisle seat nearby.

Even in this hallowed atmosphere Benedict exuded a virility and strength that made all the other men pale into insignificance. One glance at his narrowed eyes, a brief sight of his sensual mouth, the side faintly quirked, and her whole body was alight with love.

Swiftly she averted her head, but not before she saw Sheena beside him, her hand curved possessively on his arm. Sara knew an overwhelming urge to push it away and, terrified in case her expression showed it, she focused on the flowers trembling in her hands, hugging them closer to her breasts to still the movement.

· Soon the ceremony was over, the register signed, and Colin and Ella were walking down the aisle to a fanfare of trumpets. Sara was so busy marshalling the small bridesmaids and ensuring that Ella's train wasn't trodden on, that she gave no thought to anything else, and only as the couple were whisked away to Claridge's for the reception did she become aware of a man standing close behind her. She stiffened as his hand touched her, and was backing away from it when he spoke.

She swung round, her relief at seeing Dick so great that she practically flung herself at him.

'Dick! I looked for you in church, but——'

'I was stuck behind a pillar!' He held her at arm's length. 'You're pretty as a picture, my dear. But then you always are.' His eyes scanned the crowd behind them.

'Mother's on the top step, if that's what you're wondering,' Sara teased.

'I know. I saw her, but she pretended I wasn't here!'

'You can beard her at Claridge's.'

'My plan entirely. In fact I intend popping the question today. If she turns me down, I'll enter a monastery!'

'And end up producing an album of Gregorian chants!' quipped Sara, giving him another hug. 'Good luck, Dick. I hope I'll soon be able to welcome you into the family!'

To Sara's delight, her mother accepted Dick's proposal, breathlessly confessing to her daughter that she had loved him for months.

'The trouble was,' she explained, 'I thought you and he had a thing going.'

'Whatever gave you such an idea?' asked Sara in astonishment.

'The way you behaved. You constantly talked about him and——'

'Only to bring him to your attention!'

'Yes, well, I see that now, but at the time I had the opposite impression. You've no idea how miserable I was! Loving someone and trying to hide it is the most difficult thing in the world.'

How well Sara knew it! But she dared not say so.

'It's all in the past now, Mother. From now, it'll be roses all the way for you! When are you planning to tie the knot?'

'A week today, by special licence. Dick wants to keep the whole thing low-key to avoid publicity.'

'Very wise of him,' Sara concurred. 'The tabloids would have a field day. "Record Producer Marries Mother of his Star Discovery"!'

Her mother shuddered. 'Don't say any more or you'll scare me off completely!'

'You can always live in sin!'

'*You*, maybe,' Helen James laughed. 'I'm too old in the tooth to turn my morals upside down.'

'But not your wardrobe! We must get you a highly fashionable trousseau.'

'I'll do my own getting, thank you very much.'

'At least let me buy the wedding dress. You're marrying a showbiz tycoon and you must do him proud. I fancy a Zandra Rhodes.'

'For you, poppet, not me,' said her mother firmly.

'Jean Muir, then.'

'How bossy you are!' her mother grumbled.

Wisely Sara ignored this. 'Where are you honeymooning?'

'On the yacht. It's berthed in Bermuda and we'll fly out to join it the day after we're married.' Helen James gave her daughter a searching look. 'But what's with you, darling? I know you aren't happy, though you keep denying it.'

'I'm tired, that's all.'

'What's the chance of you joining us for a few weeks?'

'On your *honeymoon*?'

'Why not? We aren't young lovebirds.'

'You could have fooled me, the way I heard you canoodling in the hall at three o'clock this morning!' Sara teased, and was thankful that in her mother's ensuing confusion, the subject of herself was forgotten.

The following Monday, Sara and a few close friends watched her mother marry Dick in a register office in Oxford, far enough from London to escape prowling news hawks, but near enough to make it an easy journey.

Afterwards they celebrated at the elegant Le Manoir, where Sara gave Dick a daughterly kiss and told him she couldn't have wished for a nicer stepfather.

'I'm your friend first and foremost,' he reminded her, and proved it a little later when she casually asked him why Benedict wasn't here.

'I didn't ask him because I knew it would spoil your day,' he explained.

'I don't dislike him that much,' she said defensively.

'You don't dislike him at all. Quite the contrary, I'd say.'

The understanding in Dick's voice destroyed Sara's defences.

'When did you guess?' she asked quietly.

'I've suspected for quite a while, but I knew definitely when you said you wanted to leave the show.' Brown eyes regarded her thoughtfully. 'Personally, I'd say Benedict isn't indifferent to *you* either, and if there's anything I can do to bring the two of you together ...'

'There isn't.'

'You're as stubborn as your mother!'

'Not stubborn,' she denied. 'Simply realistic. Benedict's attitude to life, to women, disgusts me.'

'I told you once before not to write a person off because of one mistake,' cautioned Dick. 'If you'll forgive the cliché, my dear, "to err is human, to forgive, divine".'

'Possibly. But unlike Bernhardt, I'm no divine Sarah!'

'More's the pity.'

Sara shook her head, hoping the smile on her face effectively hid her anguish.

But later that day, wandering round the empty apartment, she touched the nadir of bitterness and regret, acknowledging that even if she had been capable of overlooking Benedict's past, she still didn't have any faith in the lasting quality of a future with him. To put it bluntly, she didn't trust him. And without trust there was nothing.

Yet without Benedict there was nothing for her either. So what did the future hold?

It was a question that had niggled her for weeks, and tonight she confronted it squarely, finally accepting that no matter what carrots John or Merrit dangled in front of her, she had to set her career on a road that would lead her away from the man who held her heart in his indifferent hands. Yet how tender those hands could be, seeking out the hidden recesses of her body and arousing her to mindless, shivering ecstasy.

'Oh, Benedict!' she cried aloud, and flung herself on the settee in an agony of weeping that left her exhausted.

To her surprise, next morning she was in a state of detached calm she had not experienced for weeks, and even going into the theatre later that day and finding Benedict there could not rouse her from it.

Unfortunately the calm was slightly dented when, rounding the corner to her dressing room, she bumped full tilt into him.

'Running towards me or away from me, fair Titania?' he mocked.

'Neither.' She went to walk past him, but he barred her escape.

'How did the wedding go? You realise, of course, that you're the reason I wasn't invited!'

'Of course,' she agreed sweetly. 'Without you there, I could enjoy myself.'

'And did you?'

His question puzzled her until she remembered how deliberately she had encouraged him to believe she and Dick had had a thing going between them! But how to tell him it wasn't true without disclosing the reason for the act? She was searching for a way when he cut the ground from under her.

'You used Dick as a shield, didn't you? To protect you from my evil designs!'

Damn his perception! But thank goodness she could still manage a look of rueful amusement. 'It was the politest way I could think of to give you the brush-off.'

'Clever Titania!'

'What's with the Titania bit?' she asked irritably.

'I've decided it suits you better than angel face. Like the Bard's fairy queen, you too might wake up one morning and find you've fallen for an ass!'

'It's better than falling for a scoundrel!'

Benedict chuckled, teeth gleaming white in his tanned face. 'I'm going to miss your nasty little tongue, Sara. I may even have to ring you from New York for a fix!'

'How about a tape recording?' she suggested, and before he could reply, pushed past him and went into her dressing room.

At sight of Ada, her cheerful dresser, Sara's mood lightened. The woman was a non-stop talker, and kept up an amusing flow of theatre gossip as she bustled around setting out Sara's costumes: laying the first one over a chair and putting the others on a rack in their order of appearance.

Tying her hair back with a terry towelling bandana, Sara applied her make-up. Heavy greasepaint to turn her peaches-and-cream skin the more vivid colour of Magda's, false curls to go with her bouncy personality, and an outrageously sexy costume as befitted her outrageous background. It was a task that always soothed her, as if the clothes and make-up shielded her from the world of reality.

Tonight was no exception, and by the time she was fully dressed she was totally Benedict's tough, bewildered heroine, whose love for a man of God would turn her from a raunchy broad to a tender woman.

'Care for a cup of tea before you go on?' Ada enquired.

Before Sara could answer, Sheena barged in, her only warning a peremptory knock on the door.

'I hear congratulations are in order,' the American girl announced. 'How lucky can you get, having Dick for a stepfather! From now on you can't go anywhere but up!'

Disliking the blatant jealousy, Sara turned back to the mirror and made a pretence of refixing a false eyelash. Behind her she saw Sheena wandering around the room, and was positive this was no social call.

'Do you want something?' she asked bluntly.

'Only to say goodbye. As you know, Ella's returning to the show, and I'm leaving with Benedict in the morning.'

Convinced there was more to come, Sara waited, and almost at once had a narrow wrist—blazing with a circlet of rubies—thrust under her nose.

'His present to me,' purred Sheena. 'Isn't it sensational?'

'Sensational,' Sara agreed.

'And I didn't even hint for it!'

'That must have been difficult for you.'

Sheena laughed, so full of herself she was impervious to insult. 'Benedict's so used to avaricious women, I decided to be the opposite. And as you see, it paid off.' She stroked the bracelet. 'How do you feel about a wedding ring to match? Or do you think it would be too flashy?'

For the life of her, Sara couldn't speak, knowing what it must have felt like to be tortured on the rack.

'Or maybe a plain gold one,' Sheena went on. 'Something really old-fashioned. That'll surprise him too.'

'Are you always so calculating?'

'With Benedict, yes. Marrying him is only half the battle.'

'Aren't you scared you'll lose the other half?'

'No, darling. Once I'm his wife I'll have the legal advantage.'

Sara was sickened. Sheena made Benedict seem like an object, not the man she loved. It served him right, of course, for that was how he regarded women.

'It's time you went and stood in the wings,' said Ada artlessly, and Sara, knowing she still had ten minutes to spare, flung her a grateful glance.

'Don't worry, I'm going.' Sheena shook back her lemon-blonde hair. 'If I don't see you alone again, darling, have fun.'

As the door closed behind her, Ada said a rude word. 'Can't think what Mr Peters sees in her. Nasty bit of work, she is.'

'But beautiful.'

'Not inside she ain't. She'll lead him a right dance.' Ada came to stand behind Sara's chair. 'Lean back and let me massage your neck. You're tense as a French verb.'

Sara couldn't help chuckling. 'Where did you get *that* one from?'

'Me head!'

As plump fingers sought out the tight spots in Sara's neck, she felt her tension ease and was able to think clearly. This time tomorrow Benedict would be on the other side of the Atlantic, leaving her free to come to grips with her own life; to build a future and look for someone with whom to share it.

She closed her eyes to hold back the tears. Deciding what

to do was easy; the difficult part was implementing it. Yet unless she did, she was doomed to misery.

Like an automaton, Sara managed to go on working. The show was playing to capacity houses, yet her life was a void, suspended between yesterday and tomorrow, with today a torment of lost hopes that had to be lived through hour by anguished hour.

She knew it was wicked to think so gloomily when she had so much to be thankful for—a successful career, youth, health—yet night after night she lay wakeful, tormented by the knowledge of Benedict with Sheena; holding her, kissing her, filling her with his virility, if not his love.

Even the release of her album 'Simply Sara', which immediately climbed to number one in the charts, did little to alleviate her depression, and day by day she grew thinner, her slenderness soon turning to gauntness.

From *Variety*—the American show business paper—she learned of the accolades Benedict's musical had received on Broadway, and though no reference was made to his forthcoming marriage, she heard from Merrit—just back from seeing the New York version—that he and Sheena were inseparable.

As if lending weight to this, a gossipy article in a Sunday magazine showed the two of them relaxing by the indoor swimming pool of his rented Manhattan home. 'Golden Boy takes it easy with Golden Girl', the caption read, and Sara flung the magazine to the floor in a fury.

She was still simmering, when Barbie telephoned.

'At last I've managed to get you! Don't you ever check your answerphone for messages?'

'I forgot,' Sara said guiltily.

'Go on like that and you'll end up a hermit!'

'The idea holds fantastic appeal right now! I've had so many interviews since my album was released, I'd——'

'If you're trying to cop out of lunch, forget it!'

'Lunch?' Sara was horrified. She had no recollection of asking Barbie over, and didn't have a thing in the apartment other than a tub of cottage cheese and some milk.

'Yes, lunch,' Barbie reiterated. 'At my place, remember?'

'Oh!' Relief made Sara weak at the knees. 'I'm not even dressed, Barbie. And I'm so exhausted, would you mind if I took a rain check?'

'I most certainly would! Now get your skates on and come over here pronto! I've news for you.'

'About what?'

'You'll find out when you arrive.'

An hour later, Sara found herself being led excitedly into her friend's living room, where a brown-haired young man rose from a chair to greet her.

At sight of his freckled features and warm brown eyes, Sara stopped in her tracks, sure she had seen him somewhere before.

'Sara, this is Chris Peters,' Barbie said breathlessly. 'I believe you met each other at Benedict's.'

'So we did.' Sara gave him a smile. 'The doctor cousin.'

'Right.' Barbie didn't give him a chance to reply. 'And we're getting married!'

'Getting *what*?'

Sara stared from one to the other in astonishment. As far as she recollected, Barbie had stopped using Chris as her doctor when Benedict had walked out on her.

'When did all this happen?' she asked. 'I never even knew you were seeing each other.'

'We weren't.' Chris spoke for the first time. 'We did our courting by telephone!'

'You've lost me, I'm afraid. Either I've grown dim with age or I've missed out part of this converstion. Could you—in showbiz parlance—take it from the top, and slowly!'

Chris laughed and looked at Barbie, who pushed Sara down into a chair and knelt on a little stool beside her.

'I'm glad you used the term "showbiz", Sara, because you see it was all an act. I wanted to tell you the truth, but I couldn't, and——'

'What was an act?' Sara cut in. 'You aren't making sense.'

'Sorry. But I'm so excited I can't think straight.'

'Can't talk straight either!' Chris interpolated. 'Let *me* do the explaining, darling. You see, Sara, I was the one involved in the car accident, not Ben.'

'You?' Sara couldn't take it in. 'You mean you were in the car with him?'

'No—yes. Well, not really. What I mean is that I was in the car, but he wasn't. He was at home.' Chris rumpled his hair wildly, a gesture reminiscent of his cousin. 'My car was being serviced and Ben loaned me his Merc. Then when I had the accident, he rushed straight over and pretended *he'd* been driving it, not me.'

'Why?'

'Because of Alec.' Barbie took up the story. 'My divorce was still pending, and I was scared that if he found out I was dating my doctor, he'd make trouble for us. Might even try to get Chris struck off!'

'The Medical Council are pretty tough on doctors dating married patients,' Chris explained. 'That's why Ben came to the rescue. We were lucky the accident happened round the corner from his home, so he managed to change places with me before the police arrived.'

'You'll never know how many times I wanted to tell you the truth,' added Barbie, shamefaced, 'but Benedict swore me to secrecy.'

Sara was still too stunned to fully absorb what she was hearing. 'Couldn't you have given me a hint!' she muttered.

'No. Benedict was mad as hell with Chris for getting involved with me, and said no one—but no one—must know about us till I was free. Which I now am, thank goodness.'

'So all's well that ends well,' said Chris.

'Not for me,' Sara said. 'When I think of the horrible things I said to Benedict for jilting Barbie, I could cut my throat!'

'I'm sure he'll forgive you,' Barbie placated. 'After all, you simply judged him on the story he himself invented! And he does have a rather wild reputation—which helped!'

'Except that in this instance he was innocent!' grated Sara, by no means appeased.

'Ben's always been more innocent than the media's given him credit for,' said Chris. 'Every time he dated a girl, they'd have him dating a dozen! Even the few wild oats he sowed they turned into a bushel!'

This made Sara feel worse, though she comforted herself with the knowledge that, Barbie or no, she and Benedict couldn't have had a relationship. He might not be the devil he was painted, but he was no saint either. Witness how blatantly he had angled for an affair with her while engaged to Sheena!

'We're marrying in January,' Barbie went on, 'and Benedict's lending us his house in Malibu for a month. Isn't that wonderful of him?'

'Wonderful,' Sara echoed, wishing the afternoon were over so she could hurry back home and wallow in misery. Not for anything would she spoil this moment for her friend.

But she had reckoned without Barbie's perception, for the instant they were alone in the kitchen, laying the table for lunch, she said bluntly: 'I'm not prying into your life, Sara, but I could have sworn you fancied Benedict yourself.'

'Me and a million other women, darling. He's a very fanciable man.'

'And he fancies *you*,' Barbie persisted. 'Chris said that when he saw you there the other day, he was sure he'd interrupted something.'

'Only a rehearsal.'

'Truly? I'd hate to think our subterfuge spoiled things for the two of you.'

'Don't be daft! There was nothing to spoil.'

'Then how come you looked so distraught just before?'

'Because I was upset by the things I'd said to him,' Sara reiterated. 'And what's so awful is that he never even tried to defend himself!'

'Ben never would,' added Chris, overhearing the last part of the conversation as he came into the kitchen. 'We grew up together, and even when he was a kid he wouldn't explain his actions. He always said that if you loved someone you'd give them the benefit of the doubt.'

Chris couldn't have said anything more likely to fan Sara's guilt, for she'd never had a single doubt where Benedict was concerned! From the word go, she had judged him culpable, and her lack of faith would haunt her for years to come.

CHAPTER THIRTEEN

By the time Sara returned home, she was ready to call Benedict in New York and eat dirt. Yet to apologise by telephone—with the risk of Sheena listening in—was more than she could bear, and she decided to write to him instead.

Several wasted sheets of paper later, she gave up. It was impossible to put what she wanted to say in a letter. She had to apologise to him face to face, though when that could be was in the lap of the gods.

Fortuitously, the gods smiled, for next day a burst water main caused a flood that would close the theatre for three days. Seizing the opportunity, Merrit announced that he was taking the lead members of the cast to see the Broadway version of their show.

Everyone was delighted, and Sara most of all, for it meant she could see Benedict and write FINIS to the most heartbreaking episode in her life.

'You look like a walking ghost,' Merrit commented as he sat beside her on Concorde next day. 'It would have done you more good to have stayed home and rested. What's bugging you, Sara—unrequited love?'

'What an ungallant thing to say! I've lost weight because you're a hard taskmaster!' Deliberately she changed the subject. 'What happens when we get to New York? Will we be seeing Benedict straight away?'

'No. Not until this evening at the theatre. He's in conference all day with some film producer, so you're free to shop to your heart's content!'

Sara hadn't given a thought to shopping, but she

pretended enthusiasm and asked Merrit what stores he could recommend.

'Bergdorf and Bloomingdales, naturally. Though for my money—or rather yours—I'd head for the boutiques on Madison. Treat yourself, Sara. You deserve it.'

'I'll raid my piggy bank!'

'Why not? Let some millionaire take care of your rainy days!'

'I'll work on it!' Sara made herself smile. 'When's the great day for Benedict?'

Search me. You can ask him yourself in a few hours.'

'We aren't on those terms.'

'I bet you could have been.'

Wisely she let his comment pass, knowing that in show-business one word could all too easily become a libretto!

It was mid-morning, local time, when they arrived at New York's elegant Pierre Hotel. Sara's suite was high enough above the traffic not to be bothered by it, yet low enough for her to see the graceful forms of the bare trees in Central Park, and the mink-coated women walking their dogs along Fifth Avenue. Despite the cold, a row of horse-drawn carriages stood on Central Park South, their drivers stamping the pavement and briskly swinging their arms to keep warm.

Her living room was filled with flowers: from the hotel manager, her mother and Dick, and Benedict. But she read nothing into his bouquet other than lip service to politeness, for the note that accompanied it was written in a strange hand, and merely welcomed her to New York.

But what had she expected? For him to be on the doorstep, arms wide in greeting? Still, the flowers were in what she considered to be her personal colours of tawny-gold and russet, and she wondered if Benedict had remembered this or had left the choice entirely to the florist.

The phone rang and she rushed to answer it, heart thudding. But it was Merrit to say they would be leaving for the theatre at seven-thirty, and suggesting they meet beforehand for a snack.

'I'll have something in my room,' she said. 'After an afternoon shopping, I'll need to put my feet up for a while!'

'Suits me, love. As long as you're downstairs on time.'

Promising she would be, Sara wandered round the stores. They were truly Aladdin's caves, but nothing tempted her. In her present mood she could have been given the freedom of Tiffany's and still come away empty-handed!

At six o'clock she was in her suite, pacing the floor and wondering what to wear. Sackcloth and ashes would be appropriate, with a whip to flagellate herself!

But of course she chose the prettiest dress she possessed: a gossamer affair in the same colours as the bouquet, the silky material drifting around her like a cobweb, touching her delicate curves and floating away from them at the slightest movement.

Her hair lay like a golden cloud on her shoulders, and bravado made her more lavish than usual with her make-up, the flush on her cheeks heightening the hollows that lay beneath them, the bright red of her mouth drawing attention to the sharpened angle of chin and the stem-like fragility of her neck.

Sara's ethereal quality added to her beauty, and she was fiercely glad of it. She longed for Benedict to be aware of her, to feel the pull of attraction he had once experienced. Yet that was before he had finally committed himself to marrying Sheena, and the knowledge that the American girl would soon be his wife weighed on her like a leaden shroud as she went downstairs to meet the others.

As she entered the theatre, Merrit on one side of her and Ella and Colin on the other, she was trembling so violently she could barely walk. Luckily the crush of people around them hid her faltering steps, and by the time she reached the inner lobby, which was less crowded, she was more in control of herself.

Almost at once she saw Benedict. He seemed taller than she had recollected, probably because he was gaunter—too many sleepless nights with the inventive Sheena?—which made him appear more saturnine than ever. Yet in no way did it detract from his looks; those heart-stopping looks that could tear her heart in two.

As if aware of someone watching him, he swung round and saw her. His eyes were the one thing about him that hadn't altered. Still the same clear grey-green as her own, they regarded her with the mocking gleam she knew so well. But as they ranged slowly over her body, they lightened until they seemed almost silver.

Yet all he said as he came towards her was, 'Good to see you, Sara.'

She nodded, her mouth too dry to speak, and was delighted to hear the theatre bell summon them towards the auditorium.

Slowing his pace, Benedict dropped back a step to be beside her. 'What's been happening to you, Sara? A puff of wind could blow you away!'

'Blame it on success,' she shrugged. 'My album's number one in the charts and I've been up to my eyes with interviews. But my voice is fine, if that's what's worrying you, and we're booked three months ahead at the theatre.'

'That wasn't what I meant,' he said curtly, his eyes ranging over her again, making her heart beat so fast the delicate fabric of her bodice trembled.

Neither of them said anything further as they wended their way down the aisle, and though this wasn't the place Sara would have chosen to make her apologies to him, she was desperately anxious to get them over with.

'I saw Barbie and Chris on Sunday,' she blurted out,

looking him straight in the eye.

Not by the flicker of a lash did he give anything away. She might just as easily have told him she had brushed her teeth that morning.

'Really?' he drawled.

'Yes, really.' Her lips were so dry she had difficulty speaking. 'Why d-didn't you tell me the truth about the car crash and your phoney engagement?'

'I'm sure Chris explained the reason.'

'Of course he did, but that's beside the point. I just can't understand why you didn't say anything to me. Or didn't you trust me to keep my mouth shut?'

'Typical female reasoning,' he said drily. 'But in my terms, if one decides to keep a secret, one doesn't disclose it to *anyone*.'

'Even so, I——'

'Anyway, it's all water under the bridge, so what does it matter?'

His words were a body blow, and she was glad they had reached their seats, for her legs could not have carried her any further. She sank down gratefully, but Benedict remained standing.

'I won't watch the show with you, if you don't mind. I've a few things to do backstage. But I've booked a table for us all at Sardi's, and Carol and Sheena and some of the other cast will be joining us.'

'Good,' she managed to say, giving him a brilliant smile.

Without returning it, he walked away as the house lights dimmed.

Sara could never afterwards remember anything of what she saw. All she could think of was going to Sardi's and seeing Benedict with Sheena, and the thought was so intolerable she knew she couldn't face it.

'Feeling OK?' Colin, sitting the other side of her, and

aware of her erratic breathing, peered at her in the dimness.

'I think it's the time change,' she whispered, using the ubiquitous excuse. 'It's one in the morning for us, isn't it?'

'You've been up later than that before now!'

'Must be old age, then!'

She fought the nausea welling up in her. She was indeed feeling dreadful, but she knew the reason was jealousy; searing jealousy that was eating into her soul like rust into iron.

'I'm going back to the hotel,' she murmured. 'Please make my excuses to the others.'

'But——'

'I can't stay. If I do, I'll spoil the evening for everyone.'

'All right then, I'll take you back.'

'It isn't necessary. I don't want anyone to know I've gone. Please, Colin, do as I say.'

'At least let me see you to a cab.'

'No. Stay where you are.'

Quietly she rose and made her way up the aisle. There was still half an hour to go before the finale, but already taxis were lining up outside the theatre. Climbing into one, she gave the name of her hotel and huddled back in the seat.

Meeting Benedict again had been worse than she had expected, his indifference confirming what common sense had warned her; that he had forgotten her far more quickly than she would ever forget him.

Seeing Sheena on stage hadn't helped either, for it had stirred up memories she had resolutely banked down: of Benedict lying in sexual abandon with the girl, her bright blonde hair splayed upon his dark chest, her pale limbs entwined with his tanned ones, his strong hands moving over her soft white skin to seek out the warm, inner source of her passion.

With a moan Sara cupped her head in her hands, rocking

back and forth in anguish.

'You OK, lady?' the taxi-driver slowed down and glanced over his shoulder.

'I'm fine,' she mumbled. 'I—er—I just have a headache.'

In front of her Fifth Avenue loomed, appearing wider now that the rush of evening traffic had lessened. On her left lay the Pierre, its uniformed concierge standing under the cream and brown awning. The thought of returning to her suite filled her with panic, for, once there, she was contactable, and Merrit or Colin might take it into their head to come and see how she was!

'Drive on,' she ordered. 'Give me a tour of the city.'

'You won't see much this time of night.'

'I don't care. I just don't fancy going back to the hotel yet. Show me Chinatown and—and Greenwich Village.'

Scratching his head, the taxi driver did as ordered, and it was some two hours later before Sara walked through the long, narrow lobby of the Pierre towards the elevators.

She was stepping into one when she heard the sound of a piano. The music had a haunting quality which matched her mood, and though she did not recognise the tune, it drew her like a magnet.

Apologising to the liftman, she walked out of the elevator and entered a circular-shaped room set with tables.

To one side stood a baby grand, the open lid hiding the pianist from view. How well he played! Mournful cadenzas trembled in the air like sobs, then a liquid shower of notes—like cascading tears—followed them. Mesmerised, Sara walked round the side of the piano.

Beautifully shaped hands moved over the keys, skin dark against the white shirt cuffs. Her eyes travelled upwards to the clearly etched profile, and she felt no surprise as she recognised it.

Benedict.

Although he couldn't have been unaware of her presence

he gave no sign of it, and continued playing until the song came to an end. Only then did he lift his head and look at her, his expression sombre.

'I've been waiting for you, Sara.'

'I'm sorry. I thought you'd be at Sardi's with the others.'

'You weren't there, so I left.'

'Why?'

Without replying, he rose. 'Where can we talk?'

'Talk?' she echoed.

'Yes. Privately.'

The thought of being alone with him was intolerable. 'It's too late for us to talk now. Nearly five in the morning for me! Can't it wait till tomorrow?' By then she'd have changed her flight ticket and be on her way back to London.

'It can't wait,' he said. 'And for your information, I'm exhausted too. Do you think *I* slept last night?'

Gripping her arm, he propelled her towards the elevator. She had to run to keep up with him, and as she did, the walls seemed to close in on her.

'*Please!*' she gasped. 'I—I think I'm going to faint.'

He stopped so abruptly that she knocked into him. 'My God,' he said jerkily, 'you really are ill!'

'Hungry,' she whispered, and sank into a whirling black abyss.

She opened her eyes to find herself on the settee in her sitting room, with Benedict bending over her, a glass of brandy pressed to her lips.

'No,' she muttered weakly, trying to push it away. 'I hate brandy!'

'Too bad! Drink it, Sara.'

She took a sip, trying to ignore his closeness and the warm, tangy smell of him that filled her nostrils and seemed to seep into her very bones.

'When did you last eat?' he demanded.

'Yesterday.'

'No wonder you passed out! Finish the brandy and lie
still.'

Mutely she did as ordered. The faintness had gone, but
she felt weak as a kitten and had no desire to talk. Nor did
Benedict, it seemed, for after he had spoken to Room
Service, he sat silently in the chair opposite her, his long
legs stretched out in front of him, his expression remote.

In the distance she heard the wail of a police car, the
excited sound reminding her of *Kojak* and *Hill Street Blues*.
Strange to think she was finally in New York, sitting in a
three-hundred-pounds-a-night suite with one of the most
celebrated contemporary composers; while a mile away at
Sardi's a star-studded table awaited his presence.

'You shouldn't be here with me.' Sitting up, she gingerly
swung her feet to the ground. 'Everyone will be furious
with me for keeping you.'

'You should have thought of that before you walked out
of the theatre.'

'I felt ill.'

'You mean you felt your guilty conscience!'

The arrival of a waiter with an electrically heated trolley
from which he produced an omelette, hot buttered toast
and coffee, saved her from replying.

'Get that inside you,' Benedict ordered as the man left.
'I've a few things to say and I don't fancy you passing out on
me!'

His peremptory tone increased her agitation, and with
shaking hands she picked up her fork. At first she had no
appetite, but after a few mouthfuls she felt hungry and
tackled the food with greater vigour.

As if not wishing to make her self-conscious, Benedict
wandered over to the window and stared out into the
darkness, not turning round until he heard the sound of her
cup being replaced on its saucer.

'Better?' he asked, remaining where he was.

'Much, thanks.' She rose, and only then caught sight of herself in the mirror. What a sight she looked! Her hair was tousled, her skin ashen, and her mascara had run, leaving dark smudges beneath her eyes.

'I do wish you—you'd go to Sardi's,' she reiterated jerkily. 'I'm fine—honestly. It was silly of you to worry about me.'

'Silly?' he snarled, coming towards her so menacingly she shrank back. 'You arrive at the theatre looking like a corpse, walk out half-way through, saying you're ill and are going back to the hotel, yet when I rush round to see you, you've disappeared! And you have the nerve to say I'm silly for worrying about you?'

'Yes!' she cried. 'You're making a fuss over nothing. I'm perfectly capable of taking care of myself.'

'And still capable of putting on an act, it seems.'

'An act?'

'Don't bother giving me that innocent look of yours!' he grated. 'You know exactly what I mean. You're not indifferent to me—you never *have* been. You want me as much as I want you, and I'm going to make you admit it if it's the last thing I do!'

Want! Was that the only word he knew where women were concerned? Not 'love' or 'need' or 'caring'. Just 'want'. She was wondering what to say to him, when he spoke again.

'Tell me,' he went on raggedly, 'how did you feel when you discovered my cousin was the man in Barbie's life—not me?'

His question caught her unawares, and she floundered helplessly. 'I—I couldn't believe it. That you were willing to run such a risk, I mean. If the police had prosecuted you for dangerous driving you could have gone to prison.'

'There was never any chance of that. The other driver

was totally at fault.'

'But what if they'd found out it was Chris in the car, not you? You could have been had up for perjury!'

'It was a risk I had to take. If I'd let Chris carry the can, it might have put paid to his career. Don't dramatise what I did, Sara. It wasn't so heroic.'

'Yes, it was. Heroic and stupid. Not that I've any right to talk of stupidity when I think of the way I behaved ... the horrible things I said to you ...' Her tears spilled over. 'Saying sorry seems so inadequate.'

'It will do for now,' he said drily. 'Though I admit there were times when I could cheerfully have strangled you! I didn't object to you seeing me as some kind of super-stud, but I sure as hell hated you thinking I was the sort of man who could walk out on a girl when she was in hospital.'

Shamed though she was, Sara still had to defend herself. 'Why didn't you at least carry on the engagement a bit longer? Leaving Barbie the way you did gave you a rotten name for nothing.'

'Only as far as you were concerned! You see, I'd no idea Barbie had told you she'd been in love with me. Our "engagement" was dreamed up as an extra bit of window-dressing to convince the police I was in the car with her. It wasn't meant for anyone else's ears.'

'If only you'd told me the truth,' Sara repeated.

'It wasn't my secret to risk.' A dark eyebrow quirked. 'But now you know it, where do we go from here?'

Staring intently into his face, Sara remembered everything Chris had said about Benedict's integrity. Would such a man proposition one woman while engaged to another? Far better to doubt Sheena's integrity than the man who stood in front of her, watching her from wary eyes.

'Sheena said you—you were lovers,' she muttered.

'That's true.'

Jealousy stabbed like a knife and Sara tried to ignore it.

'She also showed me the bracelet you gave her as an engagement present, and said you were going to marry her.'

'*Were* or are?'

It was a tricky question, and Sara knew her future depended on her answer.

'Were,' she said slowly. 'If you still intended doing so, you wouldn't be here with me now.'

'Are you sure? You're very beddable, angel face, and I'm a renowned rake.'

'A garden rake!' she retorted, moving a step closer to him. 'I won't have you malign the man I love!'

There, she'd said the word, even though *he* hadn't. But what price pride now they were together and he was looking at her like a starving man at a feast?

'Oh, Sara!' he groaned, pulling her into his arms and holding her so tightly she was afraid he would crush her.

Surprisingly he did not kiss her, but moved his hands shakily over her, caressing her shoulders, running them down the length of her back, stroking her breasts; almost as if he were blind and trying to get a sensory picture of her body.

'If only you knew how I've ached to do this,' he said throatily. 'How I've dreamed of holding you in my arms and woken up to find them empty!'

'Me too,' she whispered, aching to surrender to him, to become part of his life for as long as he desired her. Yet even as her arms came round his neck, he unclasped them and drew her down on to the settee.

'There are still a few things I'd like to say, darling.'

'It isn't necessary. I don't need to hear any more explanations. We're together and——'

'About Sheena,' he went on, ignoring her, and Sara fell instantly silent. 'I have never, at any time, asked her to marry me. The bracelet was a gift from Merrit and myself.

We gave one to Carol too. As to my saying we were lovers, the accent was on "were". Since that weekend on Dick's yacht, I've lived like a monk!'

Happiness coursed through Sara and she made no attempt to hide it. 'I'm so glad, Benedict. The thought of you with another woman was agony!'

'Good. You deserved to suffer!' He raised her hand to his lips and nibbled her fingers. 'From now on, you'll be the only woman in my life. And that's something I've never said before. There's just one other thing.'

'Yes?' She waited, fearful of what he had to say.

'You'll have to make an honest man of me first!'

'Oh, Benedict!' She flung herself upon him. 'Yes, yes, yes! The sooner the better.'

'Next week in London?'

Her glowing face was answer enough, and laughing, they came together again. Sara rested her head on his chest and felt the slow, steady beat of his heart, knowing it was as steady as the love he professed for her.

'Your poor musical,' she whispered. 'I'm afraid there'll have to be another change of cast.'

'Why?'

'Because I don't fancy spending half my life in the theatre, away from you.'

'Don't make any final decisions, sweetheart. Marriage is a partnership and we must both be fulfilled in it.'

'You'll fulfil me enough, Benedict. You and our children.'

She felt a tremor run through him, then the rising tide of his passion, which her own surged forward to meet as she lifted her mouth to his.

He had kissed her many times before, always with desire, but now he kissed her with reverence. Knowing this was the man with whom she would share her life, Sara gave herself to him willingly, her lips parting wide, her tongue caressing his. Aware that he was holding himself in check, she lowered her hands to touch his hard thigh, moving across the whipcord muscles to the throbbing swell he could not hide.

With a convulsive gasp, his restraint vanished, and with rough tenderness he undid her dress and let his tongue wander at will along the pure line of her throat, nuzzling the curve of her shoulder, encircling her nipples and sucking them between teeth and tongue until the constant pull on the tender nubs sent desire spiralling downwards to her rounded belly, before it centred on the palpitating core between her thighs.

With a moan she fell back on the settee, pulling Benedict down with her and feverishly holding him tight, knowing nothing must separate them; that he was hers and that she needed the total fulfilment of his entry to make her his for all time.

'Touch me,' he gasped. 'Sara, touch me!'

Willingly she did, stroking his manhood as delicately as he was stroking her. What delight to know her closeness affected him so deeply, turning a strong man into a pleading lover whom only she could satisfy. His skin was hot and damp to her touch, his body quivering as her fingers continued arousing him.

His mouth sought hers again, but a sudden imp of mischief made her turn her head away and still her hands.

'Sara, what is it?'

His voice was a thread of sound and he raised himself slightly away from her, his eyes darkening with passion as he saw her breasts swollen from his touch, their rosy nipples still wet from his tongue.

'Did I hurt you, darling? Was I too rough?'

'No. It's just that . . . Well, I don't think it's right for us to stay here when everyone's waiting for you at Sardi's.'

'Right or wrong, that's how it's going to be. I can think of much better things to do.'

'Such as?'

'Making love to you all night—or at least for what's left of it!'

'There's always tomorrow.'

'And all our tomorrows.' Benedict rose and pulled her up with him. 'But let's begin with tonight. Let my body show you how I feel.'

'Very well,' she murmured, smiling. 'Show me!'

'I thought you'd never ask!'

Hand clasped in hand, they went into the bedroom and closed the door.

ATTRACTIVE, SPACE SAVING BOOK RACK

Display your most prized novels on this handsome and sturdy book rack. The hand-rubbed walnut finish will blend into your library decor with quiet elegance, providing a practical organizer for your favorite hard-or soft-covered books.

Only $9.95

Approximately 16" x 8" when assembled

Assembles in seconds!

To order, rush your name, address and zip code, along with a check or money order for $10.70* ($9.95 plus 75¢ postage and handling) payable to *Harlequin Reader Service*:

Harlequin Reader Service
Book Rack Offer
901 Fuhrmann Blvd.
P.O. Box 1396
Buffalo, NY 14269-1396

Offer not available in Canada.

*New York and Iowa residents add appropriate sales tax.

BKR-1A

*Exciting, adventurous, sensual stories
of love long ago*

On Sale Now:

SATAN'S ANGEL by Kristin James

*Slater was the law in a land that was as wild and untamed
as he was himself, but all that changed when he met
Victoria Stafford. She had been raised to be a lady, but
that didn't mean she had no will of her own. Their search
for her kidnapped cousin brought them together, but they
were too much alike for the course of true love to run
smooth.*

PRIVATE TREATY by Kathleen Eagle

*When Jacob Black Hawk rescued schoolteacher
Carolina Hammond from a furious thunderstorm, he
swept her off her feet in every sense of the word, and she
knew that he was the only man who would ever make her
feel that way. But society had put barriers between them
that only the most powerful and overwhelming love could
overcome...*

Look for them wherever Harlequin books are sold.

Temptation™

TEMPTATION WILL BE
EVEN HARDER TO RESIST...

In September, Temptation is presenting a sophisticated new face to the world. A fresh look that truly brings Harlequin's most intimate romances into focus.

What's more, all-time favorite authors Barbara Delinsky, Rita Clay Estrada, Jayne Ann Krentz and Vicki Lewis Thompson will join forces to help us celebrate. The result? A very special quartet of Temptations...

- **Four striking covers**
- **Four stellar authors**
- **Four sensual love stories**
- **Four variations on one spellbinding theme**

All in one great month! Give in to Temptation in September.

Take 4 best-selling love stories FREE
Plus get a FREE surprise gift!

Lynda Ward's

Leap the Moon

... the continuing saga of *The Welles Family*

You've already met Elaine Welles, the oldest daughter of powerful tycoon Burton Welles, in Superromance #317, *Race the Sun*. You cheered her on as she threw off the shackles of her heritage and won the love of her life, Ruy de Areias.

Now it's her sister's turn. Jennie Welles is the drop-dead-gorgeous, most rebellious Welles sister, and she's determined to live life her way—and flaunt it in her father's face.

When she meets Griffin Stark, however, she learns there's more to life than glamour and independence. She learns about kindness, compassion and sharing. One nagging question remains: is she good enough for a man like Griffin? Her father certainly doesn't think so....

Leap the Moon ... a Harlequin Superromance coming to you in August. Don't miss it!

LYNDA-1B